"Why
And

Jake asked, surprising himself, because he hadn't meant to say that. Maureen had a body that delighted him, and he'd been staring on and off at her soft mouth all night. She'd said she was innocent. He wanted to see if she really was.

Maureen felt electric tremors running down her spine. "K-kiss me?" she asked.

"Shhh," he whispered against her lips. His mouth brushed them, very gently. He didn't rush her. He was slow and tender, and he did nothing to frighten her. After a minute he felt some of the tension go out of her body. He lifted his head to look into her wide, bright eyes. That nervousness wasn't faked, he'd have bet his life on it. "You don't know how, do you?"

"N-no," she confessed miserably.

"It's all right," he said, and smiled faintly as he bent his head toward her again. "I'll teach you what you need to know."

Dear Reader:

I hope you've been enjoying 1989, our "Year of the Man" at Silhouette Desire. Every one of the twelve authors who are contributing a *Man of the Month* has created a very special someone for your reading pleasure. Each man is unique, and each author's style, plot and characterization give you a different insight into her man's story.

From January to December, 1989 will be a twelve-month extravaganza, spotlighting one book each month with special cover treatment as a tribute to the Silhouette Desire hero—our *Man of the Month*!

You'll find these men who've been created by your favorite authors irresistible. Naomi Horton's Slater McCall is indeed *A Dangerous Kind of Man*, coming this April, and love, betrayal, greed and revenge are all part of Lucy Gordon's dramatic *Vengeance Is Mine*, featuring Luke Harmon as Mr. May.

Don't let these men get away!

Yours,

Isabel Swift
Senior Editor & Editorial Coordinator

DIANA PALMER
Hoodwinked

Silhouette Desire

Published by Silhouette Books New York

America's Publisher of Contemporary Romance

SILHOUETTE BOOKS
300 East 42nd St., New York, N.Y. 10017

ISBN: 0-373-05492-0

First Silhouette Books printing April 1989

Books by Diana Palmer

Silhouette Romance

Darling Enemy #254
Roomful of Roses #301
Heart of Ice #314
Passion Flower #328
Soldier of Fortune #340
After the Music #406
Champagne Girl #436
Unlikely Lover #472
Woman Hater #532
*Calhoun #580
*Justin #592
*Tyler #604

Silhouette Special Edition

Heather's Song #33
The Australian #239

Silhouette Christmas Stories 1987

"The Humbug Man"

Silhouette Desire

The Cowboy and the Lady #12
September Morning #26
Friends and Lovers #50
Fire and Ice #80
Snow Kisses #102
Diamond Girl #110
The Rawhide Man #157
Lady Love #175
Cattleman's Choice #193
The Tender Stranger #230
Love by Proxy #252
Eye of the Tiger #271
Loveplay #289
Rawhide and Lace #306
Rage of Passion #325
Fit for a King #349
Betrayed by Love #391
Enamored #420
Reluctant Father #469
Hoodwinked #492

*Long, Tall Texans Trilogy

DIANA PALMER

is a prolific romance writer who got her start as a newspaper reporter. Accustomed to the daily deadlines of a journalist, she has no problem with writer's block. In fact, she averages a book every two months. Mother of a young son, Diana met and married her husband within one week: "It was just like something from one of my books."

For Pat Howard
With Love

One

Maureen Harris was already an hour late for work. One thing after another had conspired to ruin her morning. The washing machine in her small duplex in the suburbs had flooded, her last pair of hose had run just as she put them on, then she'd misplaced her car keys. She ran into the offices of MacFaber Corporation bare-legged with her long black hair threatening to come down from its braided bun on top of her head, her full skirt stained with coffee that she'd tried to substitute for breakfast in a drive-through place on the way.

A tall, burly man was just coming around the corner as she turned it, coffee cup still in hand. She collided with him with a loud thud, fell backward, and the coffee cup seemed to upend in slow motion, pouring its contents all over the carpet, splashing him, and splattering her skirt even more.

She sat up in the ruins of it all, quickly retrieving her wire-rimmed, trendy new glasses from the floor and sticking them on her nose so that she could see. She stared up blankly at the taciturn, very somber man in gray coveralls, her green eyes resigned. "I didn't pay my phone bill on time," she said, apropos of nothing. "The telephone company has ways of getting even, you know. They flood your washing machine, put runs in all your stockings and cause you to spill coffee and trample strange men."

He cocked a heavy eyebrow. He wasn't handsome at all. He looked more like a wrestler than a mechanic, but that was definitely a mechanic's coverall he was wearing. His dark eyes ran over her like hands, narrowing, curious, and a faint smile touched the mouth that seemed carved out of stone. It was a nice, man's mouth—wide and sexy and deliberate. He looked Roman, in fact, right down to the imposing nose and brooding brow. Maureen knew all about brooding brows; she had once taken an art class and spent long hours dreaming of imposing Romans. That had been years ago, of course, before she discovered reality and settled down to being a junior secretary in the MacFaber Corporation.

Since he didn't speak or offer a hand, she scrambled to her feet, staring miserably around at the coffee splatted all over the champagne-colored carpet. She pushed back her hair. "I'm very sorry that I ran into you. I didn't mean to. I really don't know what to do." She sighed. "Maybe I ought to quit before I'm asked to."

"How old are you?" the man in the mechanic's outfit asked. He had a gravelly voice—very deep, like rich velvet.

"I'm twenty-four," she said, faintly surprised by the question. Did he think she was too young for the job? "But usually I'm very competent."

"How long have you been here?" he asked, eyeing her suspiciously.

"Just since the month before last," she confessed. "Well, I've been here in this new building since it opened, that is. But I've worked for the corporation for six months." Since just before my parents died, she could have said, but she didn't. "I was chosen out of the typing pool to take one of the old secretaries' places. I'm very fast. I mean, my typing is very fast. Oh, dear. Do you suppose I could rush out for some sand and toss it over this stain in the carpet before someone sees . . . ?"

"Call the janitorial staff. That's what they're paid to do," he said. "You'd better get busy. MacFaber doesn't like idle employees. Or so I'm told," he added in a cold, steady tone.

She sighed. "I don't think he likes anybody. He never sticks his nose in here, anyway, so it's a good thing the company can run itself. He never comes here, they say."

Both bushy eyebrows went up. "Do tell? I thought he worked in this building?"

"So did we," she agreed. "But then, we all came up from the old engineering building when this new building was completed three months ago and they added so much new staff. The secretaries, I mean. Even Mr. MacFaber's secretary, Charlene, is new, so none of the secretarial staff has ever laid eyes on him. And Charlene gets her work through the vice president in charge of production, kind of secondhand from the big boss," she added, leaning close. "We suspect that he's disguised as the big chair in the boardroom."

"Fascinating." He cocked his head to one side. "He sounds like a figment of someone's imagination, doesn't he?" he mused, and almost smiled.

She studied him for an instant. He didn't look like a man who knew how to smile. He was big—huge, in fact. He was tall and streamlined for a big man, very commanding, with a broad face and deep-set dark eyes. His hair was straight and thick and jet black, and his wrists had a feathering of dark hair, too. She felt that he probably was that way all over, and then wondered at her sudden curiosity. She wasn't all that comfortable with men as a rule. She was rather plain, for all that she had a budding sunny personality and dressed neatly. Men hardly noticed her, even now that she had fifty dollars' worth of new makeup.

"Are you new here?" she asked shyly. "You're a mechanic, aren't you?" she added, pushing her slipping glasses back on her nose. Really, she thought miserably, the frames she'd chosen were outrageous; they sat way down on her cheekbones. If only she didn't wear glasses. If only she was beautiful and sexy...

"I'm relatively new—" he answered her earlier question "—and I'm wearing a mechanic's coverall, so that should answer your second question."

"Then you must be working on the new Faber-jet design," she said excitedly, curious at the sudden stillness of his big body when she mentioned that.

"Yes," he said noncommittally. "You're familiar with it?"

"Sort of," she said, sighing. "Nobody can figure out why it's such a lemon. The computer people ran one of those very expensive design graphics, and according to it, the modifications should produce a big improvement on the old Faber jet design. But it performed very badly on its first test flight. That's too bad. I guess it will give Peters Aviation the edge on us." They were the competition and were trying to outmaneuver MacFaber by producing the new design on their own small jet first.

"It might appear that they have the edge, but don't count on it," he said coolly. "Hadn't you better get to work?"

She flushed a little. He sounded full of authority somehow. Probably he was married and had children. He was old enough. How old? she wondered, glancing at him as she picked up her purse and the coffee cup. Middle or late thirties, definitely. He had a few gray hairs and there were lines on his face.

"I'm Maureen," she said. She shifted her feet and peeked up at him through her glasses, wishing she had Charlene's gift of gab. "What's your name?" she asked.

"Jake," he said shortly. "Excuse me. I'm late."

Jake. He didn't look like a Jake. She stared after him. He was pretty dishy—big and capable looking. And he'd made her feel different. Almost reckless. Imagine her talking to a man like that and being bold enough to ask his name. She grinned to herself. Maybe she wasn't totally helpless. It was like a milestone in her life, and she was glad that she'd decided to stay in Wichita. She'd thought that a change of scenery might bring her out of her shell and help her become independent and capable. It still might. But her newfound male co-worker hadn't seemed too interested. Not that she was surprised. She had so little luck in attracting men. Maybe it was the glasses. If she hadn't been so nearsighted without them, she might have put them back in her purse and risked talking to hat racks and potted plants.

She dashed into Arnold M. Blake's office breathlessly and sat down behind her desk. She glanced at the phone. One line was open. Thank God. Mr. Blake was at his desk. Maybe he wouldn't realize how late she was. She punched the second of the four lines and rang the janitorial department.

"Someone has spilled coffee all over your spotless carpet in the entrance," she reported with blithe innocence. "Could someone attend to it, please?"

There was a world-weary sigh on the other end. "Miss Harris?"

She swallowed. "Yes."

"No problem," came the dry reply. "Late again, are you?"

She flushed. "My washing machine flooded."

"Last time," the man's voice drawled, "it was a strawberry milk shake...."

"I'm sorry," she groaned. "It's my karma, you see. I must have been an ax murderer in a previous life."

"We'll get up the stains, don't you worry. And thanks for that bag of pralines you brought us from New Orleans," the voice added. "We all enjoyed them."

She smiled sadly. She'd had to go home for a few days to approve the sale of her parents' home. It was her last link with the old life. They'd planned to move to Wichita, Kansas, with her, but a tragic car wreck just before the move had taken their lives. She'd almost gone back herself, after that, but she had decided that a new start might help ease the pain. So she'd invested the money she'd received from the sale of her parents' home in half of a duplex in Wichita and stayed there. Since she'd already gotten her job with the MacFaber Corporation, at least she didn't have to worry about living expenses. The pralines had been an afterthought, and she was glad now that she'd thought to bring the harried janitorial staff a little sack of treats.

"Thanks." She hung up and dabbed again at her skirt. It *would* have to be light blue. Nothing was going to take that stain out.

"So there you are," Mr. Blake said from the doorway, smiling at her. "I need you to take a letter, Miss Harris."

"Yes, sir." She grabbed her pad and pen. "So sorry. I was late, and I've spilled coffee.... Everything's gone wrong..."

"No problem," he said easily. "Come in, please."

She took several letters in a row, all pertaining to the new Faber-jet design. She never paid much attention to what they contained, which was so much gibberish when he started using technical terms. She had to ask the spelling of one or two of them, but Mr. Blake was very patient and never yelled.

Joseph MacFaber, it was said, could rage like a wounded bear when he was in a bad temper. But then he was filthy rich and used to getting his own way. He spent most of his life trying to commit suicide in a variety of dangerous hobbies, from what Maureen could gather, and left his subordinates in charge of the MacFaber Aircraft Corporation in his absence. He was in Rio now, she'd heard. He'd been away for the better part of a year, getting over the death of his mother—or so they said. Mrs. MacFaber had died in a car wreck in Europe, gossip said, and MacFaber was still grieving. They said he'd been driving the car, so perhaps he was running away from his conscience. It would be a hard thing for a man to live with.

Mr. Blake finished his dictation and Maureen went back to her desk to transcribe her notes on the electronic typewriter. That was a signal for the phone to start ringing nonstop and two other secretaries to come in and ask questions that she had to ask Mr. Blake to answer.

It was almost time for lunch before she got enough of her backlog cleared away to even start on the mail. By then Mr. Blake was leaving, and she was left with a handful of letters that she could do nothing about until he came back.

She usually went to lunch herself at noon, but she felt guilty because she'd been late. So she went along to the canteen and got herself a soft drink and a chocolate bar and sat by the window alone, eating it. It wasn't nutritious, but it was filling. She was finishing the soft drink when the new mechanic sat down at a table near the middle of the room and opened his lunch pail.

Without meaning to, Maureen found herself watching him. He was so big. She wasn't used to particularly masculine men, and she usually didn't stare. But he was a dish. A real dish. She sighed, just as he looked up unexpectedly and caught her in the act. He glared at her as if he found her interest infuriating, and she flushed furiously as she quickly turned her eyes back to the window. This was absurd. Probably she'd been working too hard and her mind was disintegrating. She finished the soft drink, put the bottle up, and smiled faintly as she passed the mechanic. She meant the smile as a kind of apology, but his dark eyes only glittered more angrily.

He dropped his eyes to his coffee cup and ignored her completely. He was still wearing his cap and kept it pulled down over his face. She felt uncomfortable. He made her feel like a man chaser, and she wanted to crawl off into a corner and hide. His anger had actually hurt her.

She put thoughts of the mechanic at the back of her mind and doggedly spent the rest of the day answering the mail. Mr. Blake had a long conversation with some official, and at the end of it he wandered around, preoccupied, for the better part of an hour.

"Is something wrong, sir?" Maureen asked gently.

He glanced at her, running a hand through hair he hardly had on his balding head. "What? Oh, no, thank you, Maureen. Just a knotty problem. There'll be a government inspector here in the morning, by the way. Do try to be on time, will you?"

"Is it about the Faber-jet design change?" she asked.

He smiled grimly. "I'm afraid so. We may be in for some stormy weather from the aviation people trying to get this thing approved."

She nodded. He left for the day shortly afterward. It took Maureen until six-thirty to finish answering the mail. By the time she had put away her typewriter and straightened her desk, most of the other employees had vacated the building. As she passed MacFaber's office on her way to the time clock, she heard noises and paused.

There was a voice behind the door, a solitary voice—it was muffled, but it sounded deep and hard and demanding. Its owner was apparently talking to someone on the phone. Maureen wondered if it was the venerable J. MacFaber himself in there. Perhaps he'd returned early from Rio. She'd have to ask Charlene tomorrow. She walked on by. It wouldn't do to be caught spying outside the big boss's office. She punched her card, left it, and went out of the building.

It was a delicious spring day. A lush, green lawn stretched from the streamlined building with its glass front, and she liked the smell of young buds breaking on the trees. The parking lot was almost deserted. There was a rather beat-up-looking red-and-rust pickup truck sitting nearby. Just that and Maureen's little yellow Volkswagen. The pickup had seen better days, like her poor, battered beetle. It ran beautifully when it wanted to, but it was tempermental.

With a long sigh she got in behind the wheel. It had been a difficult day. She put the key in the ignition and turned it. Nothing happened.

"Oh, Yellow Plague," she moaned. "Why today of all days?"

She got out and opened the hood at the back of the car, kneeling down to glare at the small engine. And there was the trouble. A gummy battery terminal, eaten up with acid. She wondered if she could hit it hard enough with the heel of her shoe to unclog it.

She was considering that when she noticed the big dark mechanic standing a little distance away, studying her with what could only be described as a calculating stare.

She glanced toward him, but before she could even speak, he moved closer. "Isn't this a little obvious?" he asked with faint amusement. "First you spill coffee all over me. Now your car stalls right next to my pickup."

His pickup? She felt as if fate were out to get her. It really had been a horror of a day. And now here was this big, dishy mechanic under the impression that she was putting on an act to get his attention. It was her own fault, she supposed. To someone who didn't know her, her behavior might have seemed come-onish. And she *had* stared at him in the canteen.

"It's all right," she said quickly. "I know what to do."

"Why don't you just crank it?" he asked, eyeing her curiously. He folded his arms across his broad chest. "For future reference, I don't like come-ons. I don't have much trouble attracting women, and I sure as hell don't want you lying in wait for me every day. Clear enough?"

That was insulting, uncalled-for and surprisingly painful. Tears stung her eyes, but she blinked them away hurriedly. She got to her feet, staring at him numbly. She wasn't quite her old, feisty self. Losing both her parents at once had been a terrible blow, and she still wasn't quite recovered. Too, she'd always been sheltered. She simply didn't expect cruelty from people. It was shocking to find that, and mocking contempt, in a total stranger.

"I suppose you're justified in what you're thinking," she said quietly, "but you're quite wrong. I'm not trying to...to...come on to you. This morning was really an accident. And I have a bad battery connection that I meant to see about earlier, but I had some distractions. All I have to do is beat on it with a shoe, and I can crank it. So please don't let me detain you."

She turned back to the engine, her hands trembling with mingled hurt and confusion, took off her shoe and slammed it against the battery terminal with a sharp, angry blow. She stood up and almost collided with the mechanic.

"There does seem to be a little corrosion there," he said slowly, obviously surprised.

She didn't answer him. She didn't even look at him. She closed the hatch, got in behind the wheel and tried the key. This time it cranked.

She didn't look back as she drove off, fighting tears all the way. Horrible, arrogant, conceited man, she thought furiously, and wished she could call him what she was thinking he was.

Maureen had an active mental life. In her mind, she could be and do anything. But in real life, she was only a shadow of the person inside her. The inner Maureen could engage in verbal battles and give people the devil. But the outer Maureen, the one who seemed always to blend into the background, was a different proposition. She fumed and muttered, but she was too softhearted to argue with people. She walked away from fights. She always had.

Back at the small duplex in which she lived, she kicked off her shoes and flopped down on her worn sofa. She couldn't remember a time in her life when she'd been as weary. Everyone had bad days, she reminded herself. But hers seemed to go from bad to worse.

That ill-mannered mechanic's sarcasm had been the last straw. So he was dishy. That gave him no excuse to accuse her of chasing him, for heaven's sake. Who did he think he was? Nobody who really knew her would ever think her capable of such a thing. She smiled ruefully when she remembered that there wasn't anybody who really knew her. Only her parents, and she'd lost them. She had nobody anymore. She didn't make close friends easily because she was basically shy and introverted. She waited for other people to make the first move. But no one ever had. And that was too bad, she thought sadly, because the inner Maureen was as vivacious as Auntie Mame, as outrageous and outgoing as any comedienne, as sexy as a movie star. But she couldn't get out of Maureen's mind to tell people that she was. The reckless, devil-may-care person inside her needed only a catalyst to bring her out, but there had never been one. She dreamed of doing exciting things, and she admired people like the absent Mr. MacFaber who weren't afraid to really live their lives. But Maureen was a slow starter. In fact, she'd never really started anything, except her job.

She put on jeans and a T-shirt, brushed out her long, dark hair and went barefoot into the kitchen to cook herself a hamburger. On the way she almost tripped over Bagwell, who'd let himself out of his cage and was having a ball with her measuring spoons.

"For heaven's sake, what are you doing down there?" she fussed, bending over. "Did I forget to put the lock on the cage again?"

"Hello," the big green Amazon parrot purred up at her, spreading his wings in a flirting welcome. "How are you-u-u-u?"

"I'm fine, thank you." She extended an arm and let him climb on, pausing to pick up his spoons and put him and them back into the big brass-toned cage he occupied most of the day. "I'll let you out again when I'm through cooking. You'll singe your wings on the stove if you come too close.''

"Bad girl," Bagwell muttered, running along his perch with the spoons in his big beak. He was a yellow-naped Amazon, almost seven years old, and extremely precocious. Her parents had brought him back from a Florida vacation one year and had quickly learned that Amazon parrots were very loud. They'd given him to Maureen two years ago for company and protection, and so far he'd done well providing both. The one man she'd invited over for supper had barely escaped with all his fingers. He hadn't come back.

"You're ruining my social life," Maureen told the big green bird with a glare. "Thanks to you, I'll never get a roommate."

"I love you," he said, and made a purring parroty noise behind it.

"Flirt," she accused. She smiled, cooking her hamburger. She was using an iron pan, not her usual coated cookware. There had been an article in some bird magazine that warned bird owners about using nonstick cookware; it had said that the fumes could kill a bird. So now she cooked in enamel or iron pans. It was much messier, but safe for Bagwell.

"How about a carrot, Bagwell?" she asked the parrot.

"Carrot! Carrot!" he echoed.

She got him one out of the crisper and heated it just to room temperature in the microwave before she put it in his food dish. He took half of it in his claw and stood eating it contentedly.

"You're company, at least." She sighed, turning the hamburger one last time before taking it up. "I'm glad you're good for seventy years or so, Bagwell. If I can't have a husband, at least I've got you."

Bagwell glanced at her with green disinterest and went back to chewing his carrot.

There was a commotion out front followed by a yelling voice giving instructions. It was usually a quiet neighborhood, but that was an ominous sound. Maureen left Bagwell and went into the living room to peep out from behind the curtain. Two men were at the other half of her duplex, the one that had remained unoccupied for the past six weeks since the music lover had moved out. People tended to come and go there, because the man who owned the other half of the duplex traveled and rented it out. The last occupant had been a hard-rock fan, and Maureen hadn't been sorry to see him leave. But now she was wondering who would take his place.

She got her answer almost at once, and it seemed like fate, sure enough. A bad end to an even worse day. A big, dark man in a red-and-rust-colored pickup truck had backed into the second driveway, with what was obviously a small load of furniture.

She closed the curtain before he saw her, thanking providence that her small yellow VW was out of sight so that he wouldn't realize who his nearest neighbor was. There were other houses and apartments in the neighborhood, but none close, and there were a lot of trees separating the small duplex from the other dwellings. Maureen had liked that when she moved in, but now she was beginning to feel uncomfortable. She didn't like that big man anymore, even if he was dishy, and she was frankly irritated that she wasn't going to be able to avoid him at home. Well, maybe he'd stay inside. That way she could do her precious gardening in the plot outback without having to be observed at it.

"AAAHHH!" Bagwell screamed. "AAAHHH!"

She rushed into the kitchen, putting her finger against her lips as she tried to quiet the screaming bird. It was almost dark, and Bagwell had to do his thing at sundown. Some Amazons purred themselves to sleep, she'd heard. Bagwell wasn't one of them. He did a whole routine, from screaming to hanging upside down from the ceiling of his cage, and he wouldn't stop until he was covered.

Terrified that her unwanted new neighbor was going to burst in the door any minute to find out who was being beaten, Maureen rushed to get a cloth and threw it over the cage. When Bagwell stopped yelling his parroty head off, she'd clean out the remains of his carrots and put in fresh water and papers.

She leaned against the wall with a sigh of relief. That was when she saw the shadow against the window. She felt her knees going weak. It had to be him. The shadow was huge, and if he was at the kitchen window, that meant he could see her yellow VW, which was parked just behind the duplex.

She waited there, frozen, to see what he did. But the shadow went away almost instantly, and nobody knocked.

Maureen remained immobile for another minute. Then she went and peeked out the curtain at the back door, but there was nobody in sight. Thank God, he wasn't going to give her any trouble.

But if he was a peace-loving man, Bagwell might give him some. The last occupant, while loud, had at least not complained about Bagwell. Maureen had a feeling that this new lodger wasn't fond of noise, musical or otherwise. It could present some problems.

She made herself a sandwich and some coffee and finally uncovered Bagwell. He was nodding off, his eyes closed, his feathers ruffled, one leg pulled up under him.

"Loudmouth," she muttered.

He was purring to himself, making little singing noises that had amused her last boyfriend until Bagwell had tried to make dessert out of his fingers.

She sipped her coffee, wondering what she was going to do now that her new enemy had become her neighbor. What a horrible turn of events. It was such a wild coincidence, to have him living next door, out of all the apartments and houses vacant in the city. For just a minute, she thought about going next door and accusing *him* of chasing *her*. But she knew she'd never have the nerve. Still, how had he known about this vacant house, and did he know that she lived here? It was so curious.

She cleaned Bagwell's cage and covered him back up before she went to watch television. There wasn't much on, and she was tired. She made an early night of it, stretching lazily as she put on the long, men's pajama jacket that was all she wore to bed. It had been on sale at a department store and looked loose and comfortable. She didn't like frilly, lacy things that scratched, and she never could find a pair of women's pajamas that felt right. But this item did. She loved it, even though it brought back some bittersweet memories of a time when her parents had still been alive. Her mother had teased her about what man it belonged to, and they'd all laughed. Her parents had known that she was far too fastidious for love affairs. She was an unawakened twenty-four, a plain girl who didn't appeal to most men. She'd learned to accept that, and now she lived for her work. She had a good job and made good money, thanks to the MacFaber Corporation. She must be adept at her job, because her last boss had recommended her to Mr. Blake. She felt fortunate to be so highly thought of, when there were typists with more than her six months' experience who'd lost out on the junior secretary's job she held.

She turned out her light and lay back on the double bed, listening to the night sounds: traffic, and the occasional dog, and jets flying overhead. Closer, there was a different sound, like someone moving heavy objects around. She flushed as she realized that it must be her new neighbor. She'd never been in the other house, but probably his bedroom was right through that wall. She moved restlessly and decided that the very next day she was going to move her bed against another wall!

Two

Maureen hated her own cowardice the next morning, but she peeked around the corner before she went out her door. The last thing she wanted was a confrontation with her new neighbor, even if she did probably have to see him at work.

She got into her yellow VW, and crossing her fingers for luck, managed to crank it on the first try. She backed it out into the road and drove off, noticing with relief that the truck wasn't in the other side of the driveway. He must already have left for work.

Sure enough, when she got to the MacFaber Corporation offices, the red-and-rust pickup was already there. Maureen went quickly into the building and to the office she shared with Mr. Blake, glancing nervously around. But her new neighbor was nowhere in sight, thank God.

Mr. Blake glanced up when she took him the mail, staring at her blankly.

"The mail, sir," Maureen said, putting it in front of him on the cluttered desk.

"Yes, of course," he murmured. He seemed to be looking through her, as he did when he was preoccupied.

"Is something wrong, Mr. Blake?" she asked worriedly.

"No, nothing at all," he assured her, but he didn't look terribly convincing. She knew that his brother-in-law had been out on sick leave ever since the disappointing trial run of the new Faber-jet design. Maybe he was worried about the older man.

"Is your brother-in-law getting better?" she asked.

He gave her a quick, suspicious look.

"I know you must be worried about him," she said gently. "I hope he's all right."

"He's much better, thank you, Maureen," he said stiffly. "I expect he'll be back at work before very long." He moved uncomfortably, as if it bothered him to talk about personal subjects. "Get me the Radley file, if you please."

"Yes, sir." She smiled. She liked her boss, but he had seemed terribly unlike himself lately. He needed to rest more, she decided, and not worry so much. His brother-in-law, Mr. Jameson, was a much less regimented person, a mechanic with an easygoing temperament but a stubborn resistance to authority and new techniques. She smiled, thinking privately that Mr. Jameson and the new mechanic would probably butt heads pretty quickly. It disturbed her to think about her disagreeable new neighbor.

She took Mr. Blake the file and went back to her routine. She enjoyed her job, but it could get hectic, especially when there were visiting dignitaries or government inspectors around. There was a lot of concern about the disappointing first test flight of the corporation's Faber jet, and perhaps that was at the root of Mr. Blake's nervousness. Quality control was where the buck stopped when anything went wong with new designs, especially when the design department could prove that they weren't at fault. That put not only Maureen's boss but the entire quality-control department on the firing line.

The design department had already proved itself blameless; they'd shown a computer-graphics presentation of the craft's performance on paper. The plane should have flown perfectly. So now everybody was beginning to think that the flaw was much more likely the result of sabotage than a design defect. MacFaber had enemies. Most successful companies and executives did. One particular rival firm, Peters Aviation, had recently made a takeover bid for MacFaber's corporation. But characteristically, old MacFaber had pulled his irons out of the fire just in time by gathering up proxies. He had three votes over what he needed to win the fight, and Peters had gone away fuming but empty-handed. But if the new design failed, and Peters got his design in ahead of time, the board of directors might vote a lack of faith in MacFaber and approve the takeover. It was a risky situation.

Maureen, like the rest of the staff, had wondered at the poor maiden performance of the renovated Faber jet. It didn't seem possible that it had been sabotaged, but the evidence was beginning to point that way. How curious that Mr. MacFaber hadn't been roaring around the place raising Cain over the difficulties. But perhaps the lady in Rio had him mesmerized.

"I'd like to mesmerize someone, just once," she muttered as she pulled up the Faber-jet file on her computer and began to type the performance report Mr. Blake had given her.

The intercom buzzed, interrupting her thoughts. "Miss Harris."

"Yes, Mr. Blake?"

"Please go down to Mr. MacFaber's office and ask Charlene for the latest figures on the cost overrun on the Faber-jet modifications," he said.

"I'll go right now."

She left the computer up and running and went down the hall to the huge office that Mr. MacFaber occupied when he was in residence. Charlene, a pretty blonde, was glaring at her computer monitor and grumbling.

"I hate computers," she said, glaring at the screen. "I hate computers, I hate companies that use computers, I even hate people who make computers!"

"Shame on you," Maureen said. "You'll upset it and it will get sick."

"Good. I hope it dies! It just ate a whole morning's work and it won't give it back!"

"Here. I'll save you. Get up." Maureen grinned at her, sat down, and within five minutes had pulled out the backup copy of the file, copied it, and put Charlene back in the chair.

Charlene stared at her suspiciously. "I don't trust people who understand how to do things like that. What if you're an enemy agent or something?"

"I can't possibly be. I don't even own a trench coat," Maureen said reasonably. "Mr. Blake wants the latest cost-overrun figures on the Faber jet. I'd have asked for them on my terminal, but I imagined you having hysterics if you had to try to send it via your modem."

Charlene's eyes narrowed. "I don't even know how to turn on the modem, if you want the truth. I never wanted this job in the first place. Computers, modems, electronic typewriters—if the pay wasn't so good, I'd leave tomor-

row. You try sitting here trying to explain to everybody
short of God that Mr. MacFaber hasn't set foot in the office for the past year. Just try. Then explain to all these
people who keep calling him that he can't be reached by
phone because he's sitting on the banks of the Amazon
contemplating the ancient Incas or something!''

"I'm really sorry," Maureen said. "But I do need the
cost-overrun figures...."

Charlene sighed. "Okay."

She got up and fumbled through her immaculate filing
cabinets until she got what she was looking for and handed
a file to Maureen. "Don't lose it and don't let it out of
your sight. Mr. Johnston will kill me if it vanishes."

"You know very well the vice president in charge of
production worships the ground you walk on."

Charlene smiled smugly. "Yes, I do know. If he doesn't
watch out, I'll have him in front of a minister. He's sexy."

"I think so, too, but we can't all look like you," Maureen told her. "Some of us have to look like me."

"I like your new hairdo and makeup," Charlene said
kindly.

"I'm still going home alone, though." Maureen
shrugged. "Maybe someday I'll get lucky." She glanced
around the plush, carpeted office. "Have you ever seen
your boss?"

"Once, at a dead run, when I first got this promotion
three months ago. Mostly I get memos and phone calls and
relayed messages. He's not bad looking, I guess. A bit old
for my taste. Graying around the edges, you know, and a
little on the heavy side. Too much high living, I suppose."
She frowned. "Although it could have been that bulky
coat he was wearing." She shrugged. "He had on dark
glasses and a hat—I wouldn't know him in a police
lineup."

"You'd think his picture would be around here some-where, wouldn't you, since it's a family corporation," Maureen remarked.

"There was a picture, but it didn't come over with the stuff from the old building, God knows why." Charlene sighed. "Bring that file back when you finish, okay?"

"Okay. Thanks."

She took the file back to Mr. Blake and sat down at her computer again. Odd, some of the figures looked differ-ent. But a quick glance at the sheet she'd been copying from told her that they were correct. With a tiny shrug she got back to work.

The canteen was full when she got there. She'd long since decided that rushing out to a restaurant was wasted time, and fighting the hectic traffic just killed her appe-tite. Even if the canteen food was artificial tasting, it was handy and cheap.

She bought herself a cold meat sandwich and a diet soft drink and sat down as close to the window as she could get. She felt self-conscious around all these people, most of whom were men, although nothing about her clothes was the least bit provocative. She was wearing a beige suit and pink blouse, with her hair in a neat French twist at her nape. She looked young and elegant and not too unat-tractive, she thought. The makeup did help, but nothing would change the fact that she wore glasses. She'd tried contact lenses, but she'd grown allergic to them and kept getting eye infections, so she'd given up. Anyway, she was never going to be a raving beauty. As if that mattered. None of the men around here ever looked at her, anyway.

She munched on her sandwich, watching the antics of a squirrel in the big shade tree next to the canteen with a faint smile. It took a minute for her to realize that she wasn't alone anymore. A shadow fell across her as the big, dark man she'd met yesterday sat down two seats away with his lunch pail, glancing coldly at her as he opened it.

She didn't look back. She'd already had enough of his arrogance. Her sandwich began to taste like cardboard, but she didn't let him know it.

"You work for Blake, don't you?" he asked.

She kept her eyes on her sandwich. "Yes."

He put his sandwich in a wrapper on the table and opened a thermos to pour some of its contents into a cup. "Does it pay pretty good?"

"I get by." She was feeling more nervous by the minute. Her hands trembled on her sandwich, and he saw it and frowned.

He glanced her way with coal-black eyes that seemed to see every pore in her skin. "I'll bet you do," he replied. "You don't dress like a penniless secretary."

That was vaguely insulting. She almost told him that she bought her clothes at a nearly-new store that specialized in low prices and high quality, but he was a stranger. Not only that, he was an arrogant and rude stranger, and she didn't like his insinuations.

"If you'll excuse me, I have to get back to work," she murmured, averting her face.

"What do you people in quality control do?" he asked coldly, watching her. "If you did your job properly, that new jet wouldn't have embarrassed the company on its first test flight."

She colored delicately and wished she could escape. He made her feel guilty and she almost apologized. He was the most intimidating man she'd ever met. "Mr.—Mr. Blake works very hard," she protested. "Maybe it was a mechanical problem," she added with bravado. "You're a mechanic, aren't you?"

She hadn't raised her voice, but he glanced around anyway. Assured that no one was close enough to hear them, he turned his attention back to Maureen.

His eyes narrowed. "That's one reason I was surprised by your very obvious attempt to concoct an engine problem yesterday for my benefit," he said.

"I told you, I had a corroded battery cable, and I didn't have to concoct it. You saw the corrosion yourself." She clasped her hands nervously. "I think you're very conceited...."

It was like waving a red flag at a bull, she thought, fascinated by the black lightning flashing in his eyes.

"I've had that dead-battery routine pulled on me before," he interrupted curtly.

She started moving away. "I don't pull routines. And I can change the oil and spark plugs, and even change a fan belt if I have to."

"A woman of accomplishments," he said. His eyes narrowed, calculating. "You know something about engines, then?"

"About Volkswagen engines, yes," she said. "My uncle was chief mechanic at an import shop for years. He taught me." She lifted her chin. He brought out something deeply buried in her—a temper she didn't know she had. She felt her face going hot and her hands trembling, but she couldn't keep quiet any longer. "And just to set the record straight, you appeal to me about as much as this sandwich did." She waved it at him.

He lifted an eyebrow, and there was something almost sensual in the set of his wide, chiseled mouth. "Odd. I've been told that I don't taste half-bad."

She didn't know if he was joking or not. Probably not. He wasn't smiling, and his face was like stone. It didn't matter, anyway; she wanted nothing else to do with him.

She turned and left the canteen quickly, on legs that threatened to fold up under her. He'd ruined her lunch and the rest of the day. She'd never talked angrily to anyone in her life. He was really bringing out her latent beastly qualities, she thought, and almost laughed at the way she'd bristled. That would have amused her father and mother. The thought made her sad. She quickened her steps back to the office.

Mr. Blake had more correspondence for her to cope with after lunch, and again she was late leaving the office. But this time, thank God, the red-and-rust-colored pickup truck was missing from the parking lot, so she climbed gratefully into her small car and went home.

Bagwell was playing with a lava rock on a chain when she went in through the back door, but he dropped it the minute he spotted her and began to dance and prance and purr.

"Pretty girl!" he cooed. "Pretty girl! Hello!"

"Hi, Bagwell." She smiled, stopping by the cage to unfasten it and let him out. He climbed onto the overhead perch and ruffled his feathers, tolerating her affectionate hand on his green head for a minute before he tried to make a meal of it.

"Vicious bird," she muttered, grinning. "Biting the hand that feeds you. How about some apple?"

"Ap-ple," he agreed. "Ap-ple."

She put down her purse, kicked off her shoes with a sigh, and shared a tart, crunchy Granny Smith with him. "Bagwell, the days get longer and longer. I think I need a change of scenery."

"Good ap-ple," he murmured, preoccupied with the slice of fruit he was holding in his claw.

"You've got a one-track mind," she said. She got up and looked in the cupboard to see what there was to eat.

"Well, it's the grocery store for me tomorrow, old fellow," she said, grimacing when she saw the meager supply of food. "I guess it's cereal or sandwiches."

She changed into jeans and a sweatshirt while he was still working on his apple. Then she brewed a pot of coffee, got out bologna and mustard and made herself a sandwich, and turned on the television, searching in vain for anything except local or national news. In desperation, she slid a science-fiction movie into the VCR her parents had given her two Christmases ago and sat back to watch it.

Unfortunately Bagwell liked the sound of high-tech fantasy weapons and could mimic them very well. But he didn't stop when they did. He continued through the dialogue, shrieking and firing and booming.

"I hate parrots," Maureen told him as she switched off the movie in self-defense.

He flew down from his perch and walked over to the sofa, pulling himself up by his beak to stand on the arm of the rickety, worn piece of secondhand furniture.

"I'm pretty," he said.

She scratched his head lovingly. "Yes, you are, precious," she agreed with a smile. She leaned back and he climbed onto her jeans-clad leg. Seconds later, he was fluffed up with one foot drawn under him, half-asleep.

"Hey, now, no dozing," she teased. She got him on her forearm and carried him to his cage. He dozed on while she cleaned it and put in fresh water. Then she put him up for the night, covering him with a thin sheet.

He was a lot of company, but he had to have at least twelve hours of sleep or he got grumpy. So she spent most of her evenings watching television alone.

She curled up with a new book on Tudor history—a work about Henry VIII—and sipped black coffee. The man next door wasn't far from her thoughts. He irritated her more than anyone she knew, and his frankly insulting attitude in the canteen had made her angry. She'd never realized how uncomfortable it could be to have an enemy. He was her first. But she didn't know why he disliked her, and that made things worse.

She'd never mixed well. During her childhood, she'd been pretty much a loner and a misfit. Her father had been a college professor, a brilliant man who taught physics, and her equally brilliant mother had taught English at the high-school level. They'd enlarged on her school curriculum with things for her to study at home, and her well-rounded education had set her apart from her friends, who didn't understand why Maureen had her nose stuck in a book all the time. She loved to read, and she liked learning new things. But her love life suffered, along with her social life. Boys had avoided her in school, just as grown men avoided her now. Her pet interests were Plantagenet and Tudor England, and ornithology; and her idea of the perfect date was a trip to a museum. Sex was something other people had, and she didn't know a birth-control pill from an aspirin. So, she told herself, perhaps it was just as well that she wasn't a raving beauty and fascinating to men; she didn't really have the right personality to be a swinger.

A light tapping on the wall next door caught her attention. It seemed to be coming from her bedroom. She put down her book and walked into the room, but then the tapping abruptly stopped. She went nearer to the wall and studied it closely, looking for holes. Surely the new neighbor wasn't a Peeping Tom! He wasn't the kind of man for that sort of thing. Or was he? But she didn't see any holes. With a sigh that was part irritation, part frustration, she went back into the living room and back to her book. Lately, life seemed to be chock-full of obstacles.

She carried Bagwell in his cage into the bedroom with her, as she usually did, so that he wouldn't start screaming when she turned off the lights.

"I love you!" he called loudly and made a noisy round of his cage before she talked softly to him, soothing him, and covered him again. She turned out the light, still talking softly, and he muttered for a minute, then curled one leg under, fluffed up and went to sleep. She settled down with a sigh, but she was restless, tossing and turning for a long time before she found sleep. The day had upset her, and she was glad that she had a weekend to regroup.

The next day was Saturday. Once, weekends had been the most important part of Maureen's life, because she could garden and stay outdoors. But not anymore. Now she was too aware of eyes next door. She knew he was watching her. She didn't even know how, but she could feel his gaze when she went to the trash can or the clothesline. She started digging a row in her small flower bed in which to put daisies, but even in jeans and a tan tank top, she felt as if she were working in the nude. She put her implements up and went inside to do housework instead.

He left about noon. She heard the pickup backing out, and with a cry of pure joy, she rushed into the backyard and started digging with a vengeance. By the time she heard the truck return, she'd done two rows, added fertilizer and planted seed. So there, she thought victoriously as she put up her gardening tools. If I have to dig and plant at night, I'm having my flower garden!

It was ridiculous, of course, to let a neighbor interfere with her activities to that extent. She started thinking about stone walls and huge privacy fences. But they cost money, and she didn't have any to spare. It took everything she made to pay the bills; there was nothing left over for extravagance.

The rest of the day was as lonely as it usually was. She watched a movie and went to bed early. Sunday morning she got up, made breakfast and went to church. Ordinarily she would have lain out in the sun that afternoon, but not with her new neighbor in residence. His pickup truck stayed in the driveway all day. But she hadn't heard any sounds coming from his apartment, and about dark, she heard a car pull up next door. Peeking out through the curtains, she watched a Mercedes convertible let out the big, dark man just before it backed out into the road and took off.

He wasn't dressed like a mechanic. He was wearing what looked like a very expensive light tan suit and a shirt under it that almost had to be silk. She darted back from the window as he glanced in her direction. Well, well, she thought. Wasn't that one for the books? He was accusing her of dressing in an uptown way, so what would he call his own leisure clothes?

Her eyes narrowed thoughtfully. Could he possibly be the saboteur? Her heart jumped. He was new at the company. He wasn't known. He seemed to be a mechanic, but he dressed like a man with expensive tastes. Didn't saboteurs make a lot of money? He could have been hired by someone to make the plane fail. Not Mr. Peters, she decided firmly. By a curious coincidence, Mr. Peters of Peters Aviation was a member in good standing of the church she attended, and she knew he wasn't the kind of man to do something dirty like trying to undermine a competitor's product. But there were other people who might try to topple a new design—like two renegade members of MacFaber's own board of directors who'd wanted to sell out to Peters and were angry that Mr. MacFaber had blocked the plan.

She felt a surge of excitement as she considered her next move. She had the perfect opportunity to observe her next-door neighbor. Having him in proximity meant she could watch him. She could find out who his associates were, where he went, what he did. She could be—Maureen Harris, secret agent. She giggled. If only she had a trench coat.

She drifted off into a very satisfying fantasy. She'd just uncovered the saboteur and saved MacFaber's company. They were pinning a medal on her. It hurt!

She gasped, looking down to the big beak that was sinking into her sneaker.

"Bagwell!" she muttered. She offered him a shirt-clad arm and he climbed aboard with happy little mumbles. So much for fantasy, she sighed.

She carried Bagwell back to the kitchen, frowning thoughtfully. Of course, she'd have to be careful about her observation. It wouldn't do to let her sneaky neighbor see her watching him. Now she began to wonder if his moving in next door was really a coincidence, after all. Perhaps he'd known beforehand that she was Mr. Blake's secretary and thought that he might find out things about the jet from her. But that wasn't realistic, she decided with a sigh. What did she know about jet designs? She'd seen the blueprints only once, and her job involved less exciting things than the actual design of airplanes.

She pursed her lips thoughtfully. Her new neighbor might actually be a struggling mechanic, but he had some ritzy friends—if that car was anything to go by. She went to feed Bagwell, visions of trench coats and spy cameras running rampant in her bored mind. That was the trouble with living such a dull life, she told herself. It would get her into trouble one day.

The next week went by quickly, with only glimpses of her neighbor. Very cautiously, she kept an eye on him. She

found subtle ways to question people, and she found out
that his name was Jake Edwards and that he was from
Arkansas. He had excellent credentials, but he kept very
much to himself and nobody knew anything about him.

She felt guilty because of her snooping, even though she
felt a sense of accomplishment that she'd found out so
much. But her conscience and the mechanic's evident dis-
like of her made her keep out of his way as much as possible. After all, he'd already accused her once of chasing
him. God forbid that she should display any interest.

She'd started eating lunch in her office to make sure she
didn't run into him in the canteen. And the next weekend
was a repeat of the one before. She darted out to do her
gardening when he wasn't home, otherwise never ventur-
ing outside. She had a post-office box, so she didn't have
to go out to a mailbox, and she only subscribed to the
weekly paper, which came in the mail.

The only unpleasantless was when she tiptoed outside to
the trash can very early Sunday morning, with her long
hair tumbled to her waist, wearing the men's pajama top
that came to her knees. It was a shock to find her neighbor at *his* trash can, staring blatantly at her. She'd been too
embarrassed even to speak. She'd darted back into her
apartment and closed the door. After she got back from
church, she hadn't ventured out in the yard even once. She
and Bagwell had spent the day in front of the television,
watching old war movies together.

She seemed to spend her life avoiding her new neighbor, she thought ruefully. But it never occurred to her that
he'd notice, or that it would matter to him. So she got the
shock of her life the following Monday when he came into
her office at lunchtime to find her eating a bowl of canteen chili with some crackers she'd brought from home

along with a thermos of coffee. She paused with the spoon halfway to her mouth and stared at him.

He stared back. He looked even bigger at close range. He had the kind of physique that must have required some careful eating. He was enormous, but most of him seemed to be muscle. He had a broad face, almost leonine in look, with large dark eyes under a jutting brow. His eyebrows were bushy, but they suited him, like his imposing nose and square chin. He was even good-looking in a rough sort of way. He had hands like hams, and Maureen thought that she wouldn't have liked to run afoul of him if she'd been another man instead of a woman.

"Have you gone into hibernation?" he asked. He folded his arms across his massive chest and leaned back against the door with the nonchalance of a man who never doubted his instincts for an instant.

She blinked. "I beg your pardon?"

"You've been studiously avoiding me for two weeks," he replied. "Not an easy task when you're living next door to me."

"I didn't think you'd noticed," she murmured.

"That yellow car is hard to miss," he replied. "Prepared flower beds seem to appear by magic in your backyard. Clothes go up and come down under invisible hands. I never see you, or hear you except accidentally."

She put the chili down. "God forbid," she said. "I'd hate to be accused of moving next door to chase you, even if I was there first."

"You're blushing," he observed, noting her heightened color with an odd expression.

"You make me nervous," she said. She didn't look at him. "The last tenant was hardly ever home, and when he was, he was playing hard rock so loud that he didn't know what was going on around him." She sighed heavily. "I've been afraid that you'd mind Bagwell."

"Your live-in lover." He nodded. "I never see him, but I hear him," he said with a contemptuous smile.

She hated that smile. The blush got worse. "He's not my lover. He's a bird. An Amazon parrot," she said uncomfortably. "He gets noisy at dawn and dusk, but he's...he's sort of all I've got." She looked up then, her eyes wide and soft and eloquent. "I can't afford to move, and if you complain, the authorities might cause me some trouble. I can't give Bagwell up. I've had him since I graduated from high school."

He was scowling. "A parrot?"

"A yellow-naped Amazon," she confirmed. "He's seven years old and very vocal. He can even sing a little opera."

His dark eyes went over her face very slowly, as if he hadn't really looked at her before. "You're very young."

She shifted in her chair. "I am not. I'm twenty-four," she protested.

"I'm thirty-seven," he said.

He didn't look it, but she didn't dare tell him that. "Much too old for me," she said quietly, not believing a word of it. "So that ought to prove that I'm not chasing you," she added with quiet satisfaction.

He frowned. Her attitude irritated him. It had flattered him a little at first to think that she'd been interested enough to make a play for him, even though he was frankly suspicious of her. She wasn't much to look at, but she had a figure that was disturbing. Odd, that, since women had lost their attraction for him in the past few years.

"I know that you're not chasing me," he replied, much more curtly than he meant to. He wasn't that much older than she was, and she didn't have to rub it in. "You've made it obvious that you'd run a mile to avoid me."

"It wasn't like that," she murmured demurely. "I just thought ... Well, if I started hanging around the canteen and spent a lot of time working in my flower beds at home—" she shrugged "—I didn't want you to think I was trying to catch your eye. You'd already accused me of chasing you when I wasn't. I don't want any trouble."

"You don't have to garden after midnight to accomplish that," he replied with faint humor. "It's obviously something you enjoy. You don't have to give it up on my account."

"Thanks," she said, her voice soft, her eyes even softer. "I've missed digging around and planting things."

He felt guilty. Not that he had any reason to. There was every chance that she was still mixed up in this somehow. But perhaps she didn't know what was going on. She might be an innocent pawn.

He shouldered away from the door. "Don't mind me. I won't be spending weekends at the apartment very often. And the parrot won't bother me."

"Thank you," she said, and managed a nervous smile. He intimidated her.

He glanced back at her from the door, and he wasn't smiling. "Where do you go on Sunday mornings?" he asked unexpectedly.

She lifted a shoulder. "Church."

"It figures." He went out without another word, closing the door firmly behind him.

The confrontation had eased Maureen's mind a little, and gave her back a sense of freedom at home. Now, she thought, she could spy on him even better. Then she felt guilty, because he'd obviously been disturbed that he was keeping her from enjoying herself at home. He might not

be a bad man, even if he was an industrial spy or whatever.

She gave up her spying on Saturday for long enough to
enjoy some gardening. She was out just past daylight,
turning over more soil, with fertilizer and seed packages
scattered all around and gardening implements littering the
soft green grass.

It was a heavenly day, with azure skies and a faint cool
breeze. Just the right kind of day to plant glorious flowers.
She pushed back her long hair, wishing she'd had the good
sense to tie it up before she began. It would be impossible
to do anything with it now, unless she wanted to smear dirt
in it from her hands. She was getting dusty all over, from
her faded sneakers and jeans up to her blue Save The
Whales T-shirt.

She was halfway finished with her day's work when she
sat down on the small sidewalk that ran around the back
of the duplex and sipped a soft drink. She didn't hear her
big, dark neighbor until he was standing over her.

"You'll ruin your hands that way," he remarked.

She jumped, startled by his silent approach, and almost
spilled her soft drink.

"Sorry," he murmured, dropping down onto the sidewalk beside her. He smelled of expensive cologne, and he
looked pretty expensive in moccasin-leather boots, char-
coal-gray denim slacks and a designer knit shirt that was a
few shades lighter than his trousers. His hair was neatly
combed; he was freshly shaven. He looked much different
from the man she'd seen only in coveralls at work, and
now her suspicions were really aroused. No mere mechanic dressed like that.

"My ears don't work when I'm tired," she murmured,
glancing at him. "I thought you were gone on weekends."

He shrugged, pulling a cigarette out of his pocket. He lit it with steady fingers and repocketed his gold-plated lighter. "I thought I needed a day off." He looked down at her curiously, taking in the smudges of dirt and the condition of her hands. "You'll tear your nails. Why don't you wear gloves?"

"I'm an elemental person, I suppose," she mused, studying her hands. "I like the feel of the earth. Gloves are a nuisance."

"How long have you lived here?" he asked conversationally while he smoked.

"Six months, almost," she said. "Just after my parents were killed," she added, wondering why she'd told him that.

He felt an irritating compassion for her. "I know what it is to lose a parent," he said. "Both of mine are dead, too, though I didn't lose them at the same time. Any brothers or sisters?" he asked then.

She shook her head. "No. I'm pretty much alone." She glanced at him, wondering whether or not to risk asking it.

"I'm alone, too," he said, anticipating the question. He raised the cigarette to his firm mouth. "I've learned to like it."

"I can't imagine liking loneliness," she said absently, watching the sky.

"Don't you?" he questioned, smiling faintly at her surprised look. "I've never seen you leave your apartment, except on Sundays. You're always by yourself at work."

"That doesn't mean I like it— Oh, my gosh!"

She jumped up and ran into the apartment without saying why. Bagwell was on the table, helping himself to apples and pears with total disregard for neatness, taking a bite out of one and then another.

He looked up at her with pear bits dangling from his beak and a torn piece of pear in his claw. "Good!" he assured her.

"You horrible bird," she groaned. "My beautiful fruit!"

There was a faint sound from behind her that turned into a literal roar of laughter, deep and pleasant.

"This is Bagwell," she told her new neighbor.

"Hello, Bagwell," he said, moving closer to the table.

"Don't offer him a finger," she cautioned. "He considers it an invitation to lunch."

"I'll remember that." He smiled at the antics of the big green bird, who was enjoying the extra attention and showing it by spreading his tail feathers.

"He loves men," Maureen mentioned. "I think he's a she."

"Well, he's pretty," he murmured dryly.

"Pree-tty!" Bagwell agreed. "Hello. Hello!"

Jake laughed. "Smart, too."

"He thinks so," she said. She looked at the big man shyly. "Would you like something to drink? There are soft drinks, or I can make coffee."

"Good coffee?" he taunted. "I don't care for instant."

He struck her as a demanding guest, but she was lonely.

"Good coffee," she assured him. She got down the canister and made a fresh pot in her automatic drip coffee maker. "Do you have a name besides Jake?" she asked carelessly, pretending that she didn't already know.

"Jake Edwards," he said. He pulled out a chair and sat down. "You don't smoke, do you?"

"No, but I don't mind it." She started the coffee maker and found him a big blue ashtray. "Here. My dad gave it to me for Christmas, so he'd have someplace to put his ashes.'' She sighed, remembering that. It had been just after Christmas that she'd lost him and her mother.

He watched the expressions move across her face with curious, quiet eyes. ''Thanks.'' He leaned back in the chair, drawing her attention involuntarily to the breadth of his chest and the muscular strength of his arms. Where the knit shirt was open at the throat, a mass of black hair was visible, hinting at a veritable forest of it beneath it. She felt herself going warm all over. He was a sensual man. The coverall he wore at work disguised his body, but his slacks clung to long, muscular legs and narrow hips, just as the shirt outlined his broad chest, making her aware of him as she hadn't ever been of a man.

If she was watching him, the reverse was also true. He found her frankly attractive, from her long dark hair to her slightly larger than average feet. She had a grace of carriage that was rare, and a smile that was infectious. It had been a long time since he'd laughed or felt pleasure. But being around her gave him peace. She warmed him. Not only that, but he remembered vividly the glimpse he'd gotten of her not long before in her oversized pajama jacket: long, tanned legs, full breasts, her hair down to her waist. He'd dreamed of her all night, and that surprised him. He hadn't cared very much for women in the past few years. His work had become his life. Somehow, the challenges replaced tenderness, love. He'd been too busy with pushing himself to the outer edges of life to involve himself very much with people. He wasn't going to involve himself with this woman, either; but being friendly might get him close enough to find out just how involved she was with the failure of the Faber jet. He was already suspicious of Blake, and she worked for Blake. She could be a link.

He lifted the cigarette to his lips absently. "You were wearing a men's pajama top that morning," he said out loud. His dark eyes narrowed, pinning hers. "Do you have a lover?"

Three

———

Maureen stared at him. "Do I have a lover?" She laughed bitterly. "Oh, that's a good one."

That puzzled him. "I don't understand the joke," he said.

"Well, look at me," she said miserably. "I wear glasses, I'm too tall, I have the personality of a dust ruffle, and even when I try to wear trendy clothes, I still look like somebody's spinster aunt. Can't you just see me in silk and satin and lace, draped across a king-sized bed?"

She was laughing, but he wasn't. He could picture her that way, and the image was disturbing.

He lifted his cigarette to his wide mouth. "Yes, I can," he said quietly. "And stop running yourself down. There's nothing wrong with you. If you don't believe that, ask the janitorial department."

She felt her cheeks going hot. "I've, uh, caused them a lot of trouble in the past. I can't imagine that they'd give me a reference."

He laughed softly. It was a pleasant sound and, she imagined, a pretty rare one. "All the same," he replied, "they haven't forgotten the little things you've done for them. Pralines from New Orleans, cotton candy from the carnival that came through, a pot of homemade soup on the day we got snow after the New Year.... You can spill coffee on the carpet year-round and they'll drop everything to clean it up. They love you."

She colored prettily. "I felt guilty," she murmured.

"Mr. Wyman, the security guard, is another admirer," he continued, blowing out a thin cloud of smoke while he watched Bagwell finish off one last piece of pear. "You sat with his wife when she had to have an emergency appendectomy."

She cleared her throat. "He doesn't have any family out here. He and Mrs. Wyman are from Virginia...."

"You may not be Miss America, but you've got a heart, Miss Harris," he concluded, letting his gaze slide back to her face. "People like you just the way you are."

She clasped her hands and let them droop between her jeans-clad knees. It didn't occur to her at the moment to ask how he'd found out so much about her. "Well, I don't," she muttered. "I'm dull and my life is dull and mostly I bore people to death. I want to be like old Joseph MacFaber," she said, her face brightening so that she missed the look on her companion's face. "He took up hang gliding last year, did you know? He's raced cars in the Grand Prix in France and ballooned on the Eastern Seaboard. He's gone off with archaeological expeditions to Peru and Mexico and Central America. He's gone deep-sea diving with one of the Cousteau expeditions that signed on amateurs for a couple of weeks in the Bahamas, and he's lived on cattle stations in the outback in Australia. He's climbed mountains and gone on camera safaris in Africa and—"

"Good God, will you stop?" he groaned. "You're making me tired."

"Well, you do see, don't you?" she asked, with a wistful, faraway look in the green eyes behind her glasses. "That's the kind of life I wish I could live. The most adventurous thing I do in a day is to feed Bagwell a grape and risk having my finger decapitated." She sighed. "I'm twenty-four years old, and I've never done anything risky. My whole life is like a bowl of gelatin. It just lies there and congeals."

He burst out laughing. "What a description."

"It suits the situation," she murmured. "I thought coming out here to Kansas and starting over again might change things, but it didn't. I'm still the same person I was in New Orleans. I just changed the scenery. I'm the same dull stick I used to be."

"Why do you want to climb mountains and go on safari?" he asked.

She shrugged. "Because it's there?" she suggested. "I don't know. I just want to get out of my rut. I'll die one day, and I've never lived." She grimaced. "The most romantic thing I've ever done with a man was help change a tire." She threw up her hands. "No man who's seen me will risk taking me out!"

He chuckled deeply. "I don't know about that. I wouldn't mind taking you out."

She stared at him. "No. I don't need pity."

"I agree," he said easily. "I'm not offering any. You've got enough self-pity for two people as it is."

She glared. "It isn't self-pity, it's reality."

He shrugged. "Whatever. How about a movie? I like science fiction and adventure and police drama. How about you?"

She began to smile. "I like those things, too."

"Got a newspaper?"

"No," she groaned. "Only the weekly. I can't afford a daily paper."

He let out a whistle. "I haven't been here long enough to get one started. Well, we can drive around and look at the billboards."

She felt like a new penny, bright and shining. "A matinee?"

"Why not? They're wasted on kids. I hate going to pictures at night and trying to see around couples making love in the seats. The heavy breathing makes it hard to hear."

"You cynic," she accused, daring to tease him.

He smiled at her as he got to his feet. "What about your green friend there?"

"Bagwell, it's early bedtime for you tonight," she told him.

"Apple," Bagwell said and let out a war whoop when she nudged him into his cage. He began to scream.

"Now, now." She calmed him while she cleaned his cage and gave him fresh water, seeds and a vitamin additive.

"He's a pretty bird," Jake remarked.

"I think so. He's a lot of company, anyway," she replied as she covered his cage. "I don't know how I could manage without him. He's sort of my best friend."

That touched him deeply. He knew that she was rather a loner at the plant, but he hadn't realized that this was true of her private life, as well. He scowled, watching her rush around the apartment before she excused herself to change into a white sundress and tie her hair back with a ribbon.

He'd suspected her from the beginning of being involved in the problems with the Faber jet, and he still wasn't convinced that she was totally innocent. But she didn't fit the picture of a saboteur. Then he reminded himself that they rarely did. He couldn't afford to let himself get too involved with her at this stage of the game. First, he had to find out a little more about her. And what better way than to involve himself in her private life?

"I'm ready," she said, breathless as she stopped just in front of him, almost pretty in her white spike heels, white sundress with its modest rounded neckline, and white ribbon in her hair. Despite the glasses, she wasn't bad to look at, and she had great legs. She grinned at her good fortune. Imagine, having him actually ask her out. She could find out a lot about him this way. Playing the role of superspy was making her vibrate like a spring. She was having the time of her life. It was the first dangerous thing she'd ever done, and if he really was a saboteur, it was certainly that. She had one instant of apprehension, but he smiled and she relaxed. It was just a date, she told herself firmly. She wasn't going to try to handcuff him and drive him down to police headquarters. That thought comforted her a little. She could always tell Mr. Blake what she found out.

"Let's go."

He put her in the pickup truck, noticing that she didn't complain about the torn seats and the cracked dash. She smiled at him as if he'd put her in the front seat of a Rolls-Royce, and he felt a twinge of conscience. He knew for a fact that none of the women in his world would have smiled if he'd asked them to go on a date in this ancient, clattering iron rattrap. But Maureen looked as if she were actually enjoying it, and her smile wasn't a suffering one at all.

"You don't mind the pickup?" he fished.

She laughed. "Oh, not at all! My dad used to have one. Of course, it was in a lot worse shape than this one. We went on fishing trips in it and threw our tackle in the boot with the ice chest." Her eyes were dreamy. "I remember so many lazy summer days on the bayous with him and my mother. We didn't have much money when I was a child, but it never seemed to matter because we had so much fun together. Both my parents were educators," she explained belatedly. "That should give you an idea of their combined incomes."

"Yes." He put his almost finished cigarette to his lips. "Ironic, isn't it, that we pay garbagemen in the city more than we pay the people who educate our children and shape the future. Football players are paid millions to kick a pigskin ball around a stadium, but teachers are still being paid like glorified babysitters."

"You don't sound like a football fan," she said.

"I like ice hockey," he mused. "And soccer."

"You're built like a football player," she murmured shyly.

He flashed her a smile. "Believe it or not, the school I attended didn't have a football team. My father refused to let me participate in what he saw as an educational wasteland."

"You didn't participate in sports at all?" she persisted.

"I did join the wrestling team," he said with a grin. "I was school champion two years running and graduated undefeated."

Her eyes ran over his muscular, fit body. "I can understand that," she said.

"I don't have anything against sports," he added. "They're good for kids, too. They teach sportsmanship."

She hesitated. "You aren't married . . . ?"

His eyebrows arched. "When would I have the time?" he asked honestly, and then realized that in his current role, it was a particularly strange answer. "I mean," he corrected, "I've been moonlighting until just recently."

"Oh. The way you talked about children, I just wondered if you might have any of your own," she said.

He shook his head. "I haven't found anyone I wanted children with," he replied, his dark eyes narrowing as he saw images of sleek, sophisticated women whose life-styles didn't mix with diapers and baby food.

"That's sad."

"How about you?" he asked.

"I like children," she replied easily. "I don't suppose I'll ever have any of my own, but I like other people's."

"Why won't you have your own?"

"You have to get married to have kids," she said.

"Not these days."

Her green eyes searched over his profile. "Maybe other people feel that way. I don't. I had religious parents. I was raised to believe that marriage came before children."

"Or anything else," he remarked with a teasing glance.

She shrugged. "I'm not suited for this century. Maybe I was supposed to be born in ancient times and the calendar got mixed up. I think I'm really a rebel at heart, but I don't have the stomach for some of the more modern attitudes."

The cigarette in his fingers had become a fireless stub. He tossed it into the already full ashtray. "Modern attitudes aren't all that modern. Since the beginning of time, people have defied convention. It works for a percentage of the population, it doesn't work for the rest." He glanced at her. "Do what you feel comfortable doing. Don't confuse rebellion with comforming to ideas you don't even like."

"That sounds deep," she said softly.

"Does it?" He pulled into a small shopping center that boasted an indoor theater. "If you want to be a rebel, you could start by doing something outrageous."

"Such as?" she probed, smiling.

"We'll think of something," he replied dryly. He parked the truck and cut off the engine, nodding toward the theater marquee. "See anything you like?"

She did. "The science-fiction thriller. Unless you'd rather see the spy film," she said with a smile, flushing when she thought how like a spy film her own life had just become.

He shook his head. "Science fiction suits me very well."

He got out and opened her door for her, grimacing when a loose spring on the seat caught her hose and snagged it.

"Damn," he said roughly, extricating her ankle. "I'm sorry...."

"I snag a pair a day at work," she said gently. Her hand touched his lightly where it rested on the truck door. She smiled at him. "It's all right. Really."

She made him feel odd. He remembered once when one of his dates had caught her stocking on a rosebush at the front of his home, and she'd raised hell for half an hour and demanded that he buy her another pair to make up for having ruined one. But Maureen was different. Very different.

"I'll get you a new pair, anyway," he offered.

"No. You've got enough to do, paying your own bills," she said quietly. "A pair of stockings isn't going to hurt my budget."

Her thoughtfulness made him feel more guilty with every passing minute, because he was deliberately letting her think he was something he really wasn't. But he had to find out about the jet. It was his job.

"Want some popcorn?" he asked after he'd paid for the tickets and they were in the lobby.

"Yes, please. We could share a bucket of it," she hinted.

"Not the buttered kind." He chuckled. "I've just taken off fifty pounds. I don't want to put them back on."

"Unbuttered is fine. And a small cola, please."

He got their order and led the way down the darkened hall to the theater, situating them in the center section halfway down. The movie was just starting.

Maureen munched popcorn and sent shy, fascinated glances at the big man sitting beside her. It was new and thrilling to have someone take her to the movies—especially someone she really liked and wanted to be with. She was going to be sad if he turned out to be the disreputable man he might be. All the same, she hoped that this date wasn't going to be a once-in-a-lifetime day. It would break her heart to have him go back to his cold self after this. She liked him, despite his possible flaws.

On the other hand, she worried. What if he felt guilty because of the things he'd said to her at first, and this was his way of making up for it? She muddled this thought around in her brain until he'd finished the popcorn and suddenly slid his big hand around hers. She stopped worrying. The feel of his warm, rough skin against hers made it impossible for her to think at all.

Later, she couldn't remember a single scene in the movie. He walked her to her door, because it was dark by the time they'd had a hamburger in a fast-food restaurant and then gone home.

"That was fun," she said shyly. "Thank you for taking me to the movie."

"I enjoyed it, too," he replied. He meant it. He couldn't remember a date being so much fun. "Do you like to bowl?"

"I . . . well, I've never been bowling," she confessed.

"We'll go next Saturday."

Her face brightened. She could hardly believe he'd said that. It was like a dream come true. He must like her, surely, to ask her out twice in a row! Men usually left her at her door and made vague promises and ran like the devil. She forgot her spy mission in the first flush of delight at his invitation.

"I'd like that," she said, sounding and feeling breathless.

He smiled down at her. His big hand touched her cheek, very lightly. "I haven't been to a movie in a long time," he said. "I seem to have spent the past few years trying to work myself to death."

"While I've spent the past few years trying to break out of the prison I live in." She sighed. "I have a great mental life, you know. In my own mind, I'm vivacious and daring and adventurous." Her shoulders rose and fell. "It's only in the real world that I have problems."

"The real world isn't so bad," he told her. "As for breaking out of your mold, that's easier than you realize. You can be anything you want to be. All you have to do is take the first step."

"With my luck, it will be into quicksand," she mused.

"No negative thinking," he retorted. "That's a mistake a lot of people make. If you expect bad things to happen, they will. You have to start with an optimistic viewpoint."

"I don't feel very optimistic, most of the time," she said. "Maybe I jinxed the Faber jet just by going to work for the company."

"Don't be absurd," he said, but his dark eyes were steady and curious.

She glanced at him carefully. "I keep wondering why Mr. MacFaber doesn't start an investigation or something."

"Well, MacFaber's hired a private detective," he informed her carefully. "Or so I hear. I guess he's worried."

Her heart skipped. So the old man wasn't just sitting back doing nothing. She wondered who the private detective was, and if this man knew. She became suddenly perturbed, worrying about her new friend winding up in jail.

He saw that worry and misinterpreted it. So she was nervous. Good enough, he told himself. She might make a mistake and fall into the trap.

"Well . . . I'll see you Monday," she began, reluctant to say good-night.

"Why not tomorrow?" he asked, pressing his advantage. Just to make sure he could keep tabs on her, he assured himself—not because he wanted to be with her. "Are you going somewhere?"

"Just to church."

"Do you mind some company?"

She shouldn't have been shocked, but she was. He didn't, somehow, seem like a churchgoing man.

Her expression made him smile. "You're right," he confessed. "I haven't been inside a church in a long time. But it will be a change of pace for me. What faith are you?"

"Episcopal," she said.

He nodded. "I was brought up a Presbyterian, but Protestant is still Protestant. What time do we leave?"

"I go at ten-thirty. That gives me time to walk. It's only just down the street," she said, aglow with excitement.

"Suits me." He studied her in the light from her apartment, because she'd opened the door and was standing in the doorway. "Are you in a flaming rush to get in there?" He nodded, indicating her apartment.

"No..."

"Then why don't you come here and let me kiss you?" he asked, surprising himself, because he hadn't meant to say that. She had a body that delighted him, and he'd been staring on and off at her soft, pretty mouth all night. He was curious about her experience, or lack of it. She'd said she was innocent. He wanted to see if she really was.

She felt electric tremors running down her spine. "K-kiss me?" she asked.

"It's the usual custom, I believe," he murmured, moving closer. He slid a big hand around her waist and pulled her against him. "Or did you mean what you said that day—that I was too old for you?" he added, his eyes narrow and curious.

She could barely stand up, she was trembling so. "I didn't mean it," she said, her voice unsteady. "I was trying to convince you that I wasn't chasing you."

"You aren't the type to chase men," he said quietly. His hands slid around her and held her gently while his head bent toward hers.

"I know," she babbled. His breath was warm on her lips and she was almost delirious with nervous anticipation. "I've never been confident enough!"

"Shh," he whispered against her lips. His mouth brushed them, very gently. He didn't rush her. He was slow and tender, and he did nothing to frighten her. After a minute, he felt some of the tension go out of her body. Her hands were against the front of his shirt, and he felt their quick, jerky movement.

He lifted his head to look into her wide, bright eyes. That nervousness wasn't faked, he'd have bet his life on it.

She was even a little frightened of him. "You don't know how, do you?" he asked.

"N-no," she confessed miserably.

"It's all right," he said, and smiled faintly as he bent his head again. "I'll teach you what you need to know, Maureen," he bit off against her mouth.

The words went through her with a shock of pleasure. She felt his mouth biting gently at hers in slow, brief, provocative movements. His hands slid down to her hips and began to draw her against him and then put her away, in a motion that aroused her beyond belief. His experience was evident, and so was her lack of it.

"Jake," she whispered, her tone soft with fear.

"Give in to it," he whispered back. "You're safe. I won't do anything to hurt you or frighten you. Give me back the kiss, Maureen. Open your mouth a little and lift it against mine.... Yes, little one, like that.... Harder this time... harder...!"

She felt the fierce crush of his mouth with awed pleasure. He tasted of coffee and smoke, and his lips were devastatingly expert. Her arms went under his and around him; her hands savored the taut muscles of his broad shoulders. She clung to him, her body trembling with a kind of pleasure that terrified her while his hard mouth took everything it wanted from hers.

When he lifted his head, her lips followed his, but he held her by the arms and stood looking down at her with an expression she couldn't decipher.

"You're trembling," he said quietly.

"I... Nobody ever... ever kissed me that way," she stammered, embarrassed by her own lack of experience.

His eyes darkened. He couldn't have imagined even a week ago that there was a woman in the country who hadn't had at least one lover. He was astonished to discover that it mattered to him that Maureen hadn't. He moved his big hands slowly between her rib cage and her waist, enjoyed the softness of her body, the feel of her trembling hands against his shirt. Work was the last thing in his mind as he looked at her. She wasn't the only one that hard kiss had affected.

"I won't take advantage of it," he said, his voice very deep in the stillness. "You please me," he added huskily, brushing his mouth gently over her forehead. "You please me very much."

She sighed and nestled close. "I must seem terribly ignorant," she whispered. "I'm sorry."

He linked his hands behind her and swung her lightly from side to side. "Why are you sorry?" he asked. "Hasn't it occurred to you that innocence can be very exciting to a man?"

She grimaced. "Not to the few men I ever went out with. They thought I was a hopeless case."

"Their loss. My gain." He said it lightly, but his deep voice was like shades of velvet.

She looked up, her eyes sliding quietly over the broad face with its deep-set dark eyes, its imposing nose and square chin. It was a very masculine face, full of authority and strength. Somehow he didn't look like a mechanic, she thought dreamily.

"Have you always been a mechanic?" she asked absently.

He looked and felt briefly uncomfortable, and his hands stilled on her waist. "No. Not always." He let her go. "You'd better get some sleep. I'll see you in the morning."

"All right." He seemed suddenly remote, and she wondered what she'd done to cause that reaction.

He lit a cigarette, pausing on the sidewalk to look back at her. "Do you cook breakfast or eat cereal?" he asked unexpectedly.

She hesitated. "I make biscuits and eggs and sausages, usually. Do you cook?"

He shook his head and smiled ruefully. "I'm living on stale cereal."

"You could have breakfast with me," she volunteered in a rush, forcing the words out.

One dark eyebrow lifted with gentle amusement. "Could I?"

"There's always plenty. Bagwell doesn't eat much," she said, laughing.

"What time?"

She'd been holding her breath. Now she let it out, feeling as if she were floating. "Nine."

He nodded. "See you then."

She watched him go, her eyes eloquent. It wasn't a dream. It was real. She couldn't have imagined even a week ago that her worst enemy would become her friend. But it seemed to be happening, all the same. She wouldn't let herself think about what he could be. Spying was beginning to lose its thrill already. Now she was going to go through agonies worrying about him.

She was up at six the next morning, just to make sure she didn't burn the biscuits. She baked them up fluffy and light, and fried both sausages and bacon, just in case, and had to restrain herself from making the eggs much too early.

But even as she stood in the kitchen in her long blue, men's pajama top, barefoot, with her long hair around her shoulders, deliberating, there was a light tap on the back door.

Trembling with anticipation, she pulled the curtain aside and looked out. It was him, dressed in an older but still trendy gray suit, with the jacket looped carelessly over one finger, in a white shirt and a tie. She wondered idly why he hadn't worn the very expensive suit she'd seen him in just days before. Could he possibly know that she was suspicious of him, and was he, therefore, trying to alleviate her suspicions?

She opened the door without thinking and blushed when his eyes went automatically to her long, tanned legs and back up to the deep cleft between her full breasts.

"I . . . I haven't got a robe," she stammered, embarrassed.

His eyes moved up to hers, dark and steady. "You have a beautiful body," he said quietly. "It's respectably covered and I'm not a lecher."

"Oh, I didn't mean it like that," she said miserably. "It's just . . ."

He came in and closed the door, tossed his jacket onto a chair and moved toward her without ever taking his dark eyes from her face. She almost backed away, but his hands came up to her face, framing it.

"There's no need to run from me," he said quietly, searching her wide green eyes. "I'll never hurt you."

"I'm not afraid of you."

He bent, smiling, and put his hard mouth gently against hers, holding the soft kiss until she relaxed and he felt her hesitant movement toward him. Heady with her shy submission, he let his big hands move to her waist and gently brought her against him. It was fiercely arousing to feel her breasts against his chest through the thinness of his shirt and her pajama top; to know that she was nude under it.

"Come closer," he whispered into her parted lips. "Put your arms around me."

"I'm not . . . dressed," she moaned, trying to be sane.

"God, I know!" he bit off. His hands flattened on her shoulder blades, pulling, so that he could feel her breasts crush softly against his stomach because he was so much taller than she was. The feel of them made him groan.

"What?" she whispered, pulling back to look up into his dark, glittering eyes. "Did I do something wrong?"

He set his teeth, holding back the words. She wasn't like the women he'd known. He couldn't tell her that he was so aroused he felt like pushing her down on the couch and ravishing her. Her eyes were wide and misty with excitement. Her mouth was just faintly swollen where his had crushed it. She looked and felt like a woman on the verge of her first love affair, and he wanted desperately to be the man. The first man. The only man.

His hands held her waist, marveling at its smallness as he smoothed her top against her sides, watching with unnerving curiosity the taut thrust of her nipples against the fabric. She didn't even seem to be aware of that maddening little giveaway.

"I think you'd better put on some clothes," he said quietly, his eyes going back up to hers with darkening intent. "You can't imagine how tempting you look right now."

Her face changed, brightened. She smiled softly as he released her. "Do I, really?"

He turned away, his face rigid, and reached for a cigarette. "Have you already made coffee?" he asked stiffly.

She didn't quite understand his abrupt mood change. Perhaps he wasn't awake yet. "Yes. Help yourself. I'll be right back." She moved into the bedroom and closed the door, still tingling from his warm, hungry embrace. It was nice being kissed like that, and a little frightening, too. She'd felt giddy and weak and had experienced a new kind of throbbing ache inside her. What an odd reaction to a kiss, she thought, and then fumbled her way into hose, a slip and a white dress, pausing to put on a minimum of makeup and put up her hair. She looked cool and young and neat, but not beautiful. She sighed at her reflection, pushed her slipping glasses back up on her nose, and went back into the living room, carrying her white high heels and her Sunday purse with her. She tossed them onto the coffee table and padded in her stocking feet to the kitchen.

Jake was drinking black coffee at the table, and he smiled at the picture she made. She looked neat and un-ruffled, and he wanted to let her hair down and wrinkle that dress. His dark eyes said so.

She flushed, smiling at him. "Will I do?"

"Oh, yes," he responded. "You'll do."

"I'll just fix the eggs," she said, moving to get an apron. He watched her quick movements with lazy appreciation, wondering at the domestic picture she made. He'd never actually watched a woman cook before. It was fascinating. So was she.

"This is like another world to me," he remarked suddenly. "I've never felt this relaxed in my life or enjoyed a woman's company so much."

She turned to look at him, her eyes soft and excited. "Really?"

"Really. You're good for me."

She lowered her eyes shyly and went back to the eggs. "I like being with you, too, Jake."

He felt uncomfortable at the use of his nickname. He shifted in the chair. "How do you like working for Blake?" he asked suddenly.

"I like it very much," she confessed. "Except that poor Mr. Blake worries so much," she added. "He's been a bundle of nerves this week. That's not like him at all." She shrugged, unaware of her companion's intent stare. "Maybe it's this Faber-jet problem. It's made us all nervous." She glanced at him. "Do you suppose somebody could be trying to sabotage it?"

Four

———

Oh, did you burn yourself?'' Maureen exclaimed. She rushed for paper towels while Jake gritted his teeth against the pain from the sudden splash of hot black coffee on his big hand.

Her question about sabotage had caught him off guard and he'd almost given the show away with that clumsy movement. He forgot the sting of the hot liquid, though, watching her concerned face and the quick, deft movements of her slender hands as she mopped his hand and wrist and frowned over the red burn mark on the darkly tanned flesh.

It had been years since anyone had fussed over him. She didn't appear to be doing it because she wanted to impress him. She seemed genuinely to care that he'd been hurt.

She was leaning over him, her soft eyes concerned, her hands gentle as they rubbed some soothing ointment over the burn. "I'm so sorry," she said. "I must have bumped the table. I'm so clumsy—"

"I knocked the cup with my hand," he corrected. "It wasn't anything you did. What is that stuff?" he asked, frowning as he watched her rub it in, her fingers small against his huge hand.

"Antibiotic ointment," she murmured. "It's mostly for cuts and bee stings, but it's all I've got and maybe it will help."

"Do you always fuss over people like this?" he asked, his voice faintly dry.

She glanced at him. "Well, yes," she said apologetically. "I wanted to be a nurse, but I get sick if I see blood." She sighed and sat down beside him. "Who am I kidding? I've never tried to be anything except what I am. I only have an adventurous spirit. The rest of me is pure coward."

"I'd say it was lack of opportunity," he murmured, smiling at her. His eyes grew thoughtful. "When I was your age, I hired on a tramp steamer and went to the Canary Islands and Fiji and Hawaii," he said, reminiscing. "I worked on a sugarcane plantation on the big island in Hawaii, and then I worked as a clerk for one of the small airlines. I learned to surf over there. Got pretty good at it, too, despite my size," he added dryly, noticing that she was hanging on every word. "Then one of the pilots started teaching me how to fly, and I was hooked."

"Is that where you learned to work on airplanes?" she asked, her eyes curious and soft.

He hesitated. "Yes. Of course."

"It must have been very exciting. Didn't your parents mind?" she asked.

"They went through the ceiling," he recalled. "But I was used to going my own way. I wanted to see what I could do on my own. I think I surprised them as much as I surprised myself.'' His dark eyes grew serious. "You see, Maureen, it isn't enough to want things. You have to go out and get them. Dreams are fine, but only if they lead to solutions.''

"You mean I have to take chances, now and again,'' she said.

"That's part of it. You have to be willing to make sacrifices, as well,'' he added somberly. "Sometimes the sacrifices can be pretty rough. I spent most of my adult life making—'' he almost said money "—airplanes. Then one day I woke up and discovered that airplanes had become my whole life. I'd given up a private life in the process.'' His big shoulders moved against the soft fabric of his shirt. "I tried to change that. To make time for the things I used to do that I stopped doing because of work. But something was still missing.'' He looked at her quietly. "Things don't make up for people, did you know?''

"Yes,'' she said softly. Her eyes fell to his chest and she could see the dark, thick shadow under his shirt. Her lips parted as she stared at him there and wondered what was beneath that white fabric. Her own thoughts startled her, because she'd never been curious about a man's body before.

He saw that curiosity and smiled to himself. So she was thinking about him that way, was she? He was suddenly sorry that he couldn't give her what she was looking for. But an affair was out of the question with her, and so was anything more permanent. Even when this was all over, there was little possibility that she could fit into his world. She was sweet and kind, but she'd need to be a barracuda to survive what he had to contend with. There was little sense in starting something he couldn't finish.

All the same, her eyes disturbed him. She had a way of looking at him that made his heart go wild in his chest. Especially when he could see the thoughts in her unguarded face.

"I'm hairy there," he said quietly, watching her eyes register her shock. "And not just there." He leaned toward her, holding her gaze. "All over, Maureen."

The flush started at her neck and worked its way up into her cheeks and finally to her hairline. She averted her eyes and started to get up. "I'll just wash these dishes—"

His hand caught hers, holding her there while he struggled with genuine regret. Mockery and taunting arrogance were very much a part of his personality. He used them like weapons to keep his employees in line, to keep women at bay. But he hadn't meant to hurt Maureen.

"That was a low blow," he said, his eyes narrow and intent. "I didn't mean to embarrass you." He drew a deep breath. "Look, honey, it bothers me when you look at me like that, okay?" he said, opting for the truth. "You're not the kind of woman I can carry into the bedroom and amuse myself with. So don't create problems. Be the good girl you are and keep those sultry eyes to yourself."

"Sultry?" Her eyebrows arched.

He laughed helplessly at her expression. "Never mind, Goldilocks. Wash your dishes. I'll have my coffee with Bagwell. Does he need feeding?"

"I'll do it, but thanks for offering." She tidied Bagwell's cage and changed his water and fed him while her mind glowed at what Jake had said. So she disturbed him. And she had sultry eyes. She could hardly keep her secret smiles to herself after that. He might not want to complicate things, but it pleased her very much that he found her so attractive.

They went to church, and after the service they sat in a nearby McDonald's and ate hamburgers and fries.

"I enjoyed that," he said. "Going to church, I mean. I haven't had much to do with organized religion in recent years. Too busy."

"Where did you work in between Hawaii and Mac-Faber?" she asked.

It was a legitimate question, but he had to think hard for an answer. "Lockheed-Georgia," he said. "Great people. They're just north of Atlanta, in Marietta." In fact, he'd been to Lockheed-Georgia for the unveiling of the C-5A Galaxy cargo plane. Fortunately he remembered just a little about the layout.

"I had a cousin who was a draftsman there," she said unexpectedly, and he had to bite his tongue. "But he was transferred to their California plant last year," she added, and he relaxed. "I don't guess you'd have known him. He only worked there for a year."

"I guess not," he agreed.

"I wonder why I haven't seen you before?" she mused, smiling at him. "Most of the mechanics share the canteen with us."

"I was at the construction plant in Kansas City until this month," he told her. It was true enough, he'd raised hell down there. "Where the Faber-jet renovation is taking place," he added.

"Yes, we know about the other divisions, even if we haven't seen them," Maureen agreed. "It's a huge corporation, isn't it? There's the engineering plant, where we are, and the construction plant, the electronics plant... However do you suppose Mr. MacFaber keeps up with it all?"

"He has capable executives and he delegates a lot of authority," he said, adding "Probably," when she stared at him. "I've heard some of the men talk about him," he said to alleviate her suspicions.

"Charlene says he's heavy," she murmured. "And old. I wonder what he looks like? There used to be a portrait of him, Charlene said, but somebody lost it."

He pursed his lips, remembering all too well what had become of that unflattering likeness of Joseph MacFaber, but he couldn't tell her.

"How does Charlene like him?" he asked.

"She's never met him," she said. "She's only been his secretary for four months, and he's been out of the country for almost a year. He flies in occasionally, they say, but he has most of his contact with the corporation through memos and phone calls." She frowned into her coffee. "It seems kind of haphazard to me. I mean, he's the man on top. If there are design problems with his jet, you'd think he'd be here raising Cain about it instead of jumping off mountains on hang gliders. Wouldn't you?" she added, looking up to surprise a strange expression on his broad, dark face.

"Maybe he doesn't trust anybody," he suggested.

She shrugged. "You can't blame him for that. If somebody really is trying to sabotage his new design, he'd be well-advised not to." She pursed her lips. "I guess he suspects Mr. Peters, don't you?" she added thoughtfully. "But I wonder if Mr. Peters would do something like that? I know he wants to control the corporation, but he seems like a very nice man to me."

He knew he'd stopped breathing. "You know him?"

"Didn't you see him this morning?" she asked. "He goes to my church."

He didn't flick an eyelash, but he felt his head whirling. "Did he see us?"

"No, I don't think so. He was in the front pew and we left early. I would have introduced you," she added with a smile. "He's very friendly."

That, he thought with blatant relief, would have been one hell of an introduction, all right. But it raised some terrible questions. If she went to church with Peters, and knew him . . . But would people who went to church really be involved in something as unholy as sabotage? He'd learned over the years that the sweetest faces sometimes masked terrible greed.

"You look worried," she said. "Is something wrong?"

"No. Finish your coffee. We'd better go."

She didn't understand what was wrong. He drove her back to her apartment, murmured something about seeing her the next day, and left her there without a word or a smile.

Strange, unpredictable man, she thought, worried. Had she said something that made him angry? Did he think she was being disloyal to the company by talking so nicely about Mr. Peters? But the other airplane executive really was a nice man. He was ambitious, but so were a lot of other people. Then she began to wonder. Did he know Mr. Peters, and was he afraid Mr. Peters might have recognized him? That worried her. Everything about this new relationship worried her. She was beginning to think some very disturbing thoughts about her friend. She didn't want to suspect him anymore, because he was already becoming part of her life. But what if he was involved in the sabotage? If it even was sabotage, she thought comfortingly.

She spent the rest of the day watching movies with Bagwell, wondering if her new friendship had already gone the way of her others—down the tube.

Monday morning, Jake had already gone when she left for work. She'd had a lingering hope that he might ask her to ride in with him, but no invitation had been forthcoming. In fact, she hadn't seen a light on in his apartment Sunday evening, even though the truck had still been there.

He was a curious man, but she was already beginning to feel something deep and disturbing for him. He attracted her as no other man ever had, and she couldn't imagine how she was going to stay alive if he canceled their Saturday-night bowling date. It was absurd to get so involved with a stranger, she told herself, especially a stranger who'd made it clear that friendship was all he was offering. But she was lonely, and he made her feel free.

She went into Mr. Blake's office with forced cheer, only to find her boss looking as if he'd been walked over and sat on.

"Good morning?" She made a question of it unconsciously.

"It is not," he muttered. "My stupid brother-in-law is going to be the death of me!"

"Is he worse?" she asked hesitantly, because he'd been reluctant to discuss his in-law once before.

He sighed angrily and ran a hand through what there was of his dark hair. "No, he's not worse. Not yet, anyway," he added. He looked up. "Have you heard anything from Charlene about an investigation?" he asked hesitantly, as if he didn't really want to ask for gossip.

"Well...not exactly from Charlene," she said, trying to protect Jake. "But there's talk that Mr. MacFaber has hired a private investigator to see if he can find any evidence of sabotage."

Blake nodded. He sat back in his chair and loosened his tie. "Yes, I heard the same talk. I knew he wouldn't rest until he got to the bottom of it. MacFaber would follow an enemy into hell to get him, they say. I'm beginning to believe it. He can be ruthless when his corporation is involved."

"You can't blame him, sir," she replied. "It must be terribly expensive to have something go wrong with a new design."

"More expensive than we realize sometimes." He touched his desk with a careless hand. "They'll narrow it down to the mechanics, you mark my words," he murmured absently.

Maureen felt her heart skip a beat. No. It couldn't be Jake! She couldn't bear to see him arrested, disgraced, imprisoned!

"We'd better get to work," he said abruptly, sitting up straight. "Get your pad, Maureen, and we'll get the correspondence out of the way first."

"Yes, sir."

She worried all morning about Jake, and what was going to become of him when the private detective caught up with him. He would look suspicious to any logical person, especially if he were seen in his expensive casual clothing.

At lunchtime she went to the canteen, looking all around, trying to catch a glimpse of Jake, but he was nowhere to be found. She went out to the parking lot after she'd wolfed down a sandwich, and his truck was there.

There were a lot of mechanics who worked for the corporation, although not as many here at the administrative offices. There were enough to keep up the company planes, which were based here, and not so many that Maureen couldn't recognize most of them. But when she walked past the big hangars, she was too nervous to go inside and ask for Jake.

She wondered idly if he knew Mr. Blake's brother-in-law, who'd been working at the Kansas City assembly plant until his sudden illness. She'd have to remember to ask him when she saw him again.

He didn't show up the rest of the day, and when she got to her apartment, hoping that he might be home, he wasn't there, either. Two long days went by, during which Maureen became more and more certain that he'd washed his hands of her. She didn't see him at MacFaber's, and despite the continued presence of his truck there, she was reasonably sure that he wasn't working. She was too afraid to ask if he'd been fired. She didn't want to have to hear that he'd been caught by the elusive Mr. MacFaber.

Wednesday evening when she went home, there was a movie on television that she particularly wanted to see. She settled down with homemade popcorn, sharing with Bagwell, and concentrated on the screen. She was watching the mystery with such intensity that the knock on the door came twice before she heard it.

Her heart turned cartwheels as she jumped up and ran to answer it. There was only one person who might call this late at night. She smoothed down her loosened hair and cursed her lack of glamour. She was wearing jeans and a very old blue tank top, and there wasn't a speck of lipstick on her face. Oh, well. She was too glad to see him to care how she looked.

She threw open the door, her face aglow, her eyes brilliant. It was Jake, in corded tan slacks and a yellow designer knit shirt. His face was worn and tired, and he looked as if he hadn't slept in days.

"Got any coffee?" he asked with a tired smile.

She laughed. "Oh, yes," she said. "Come in!"

He moved into the kitchen, his dark eyes warm at the excitement on her face, at her obvious joy in his presence.

She might be a saboteur, he thought, but she was pure delight to be around. She brought out qualities in him of which he'd been unaware. Protectiveness. Possessiveness. Easy conversation and quiet pleasure in the simplest things. He'd found himself hoping against hope in the past few days that she was as innocent as she seemed. In another week he'd have his answer, one way or another.

"Did you miss me?" he asked, needing to hear her admit it, even though he could see it in her face.

"Yes," she confessed. Her eyes searched his with helpless hunger. "I thought you'd been... I thought you'd quit your job," she corrected.

"They sent me to another plant for a few days," he said. That was almost true. "I didn't expect to be gone for so long."

"Are you back to stay this time?" She had to know. "They aren't going to transfer you, are they?"

He chuckled deep in his throat. "I don't think there's any threat of that."

She smiled. "I'm glad." Her hands fiddled with the edge of her top as she fought for words. "I'll pour you some coffee."

"Where's Bagwell?" he asked, glancing at the empty cage.

"Watching television," she said. "Eating popcorn and probably the bowl it's in. He likes murder mysteries. He screams along with the victims," she said, laughing.

He glanced into the living room. "Amazing that he stays put like that. Most birds like to roam."

"Amazons are climbers, not fliers. And Bagwell isn't too adventurous. He's afraid of red things." She grinned. "He won't go near my Christmas plates."

"That has to be an advantage from time to time," he said.

"I suppose it is." She poured coffee into a cup, almost spilling it, and handed it to him. "Do you want to sit in here, or watch the movie with us?"

"What is it?"

She told him.

"I've seen it, but I don't mind seeing it twice." He followed her into the living room and sat down beside her on the sofa.

Bagwell giggled and jumped off onto the cushions, his head down as he made a pigeon-toed, parroty dash toward the newcomer.

"Look out, he bites," Maureen exclaimed.

But Jake just extended his brawny forearm and let Bagwell climb aboard. He swung him over to the arm of the sofa and let him off. "Stay there," he told the bird with the same authority in his voice that Maureen had heard only once or twice.

Bagwell knew the boss when he heard him. He settled down on the sofa arm with a nugget of popcorn in one claw and left well enough alone.

"How do you do that?" Maureen asked, fascinated.

He leaned back with his arm around her shoulders, as casually as if they'd known each other for a lifetime. "Years of practice yelling at subordinates," he mused, glancing down at her. "I've been shop foreman a time or two in my life," he added to keep her from asking more questions.

"Oh."

"How are things going at the office?" he asked at the next commercial.

"Fine, I suppose," she said. She looked up at him, her eyes soft and quiet on his very masculine features. He had such a strong face, she thought dreamily.

"Any new gossip?" he persisted.

"Just that they're still looking for the problem with the Faber jet," she said. "Charlene said that one of the vice presidents thinks Mr. MacFaber is on his way back. I guess he's going to start putting pressure on his private detective."

Jake looked thoughtful. "There's an idea."

"And Mr. Blake thinks it might be...someone mechanical," she said hesitantly, unwilling to come right out and say it.

He glanced down at her curiously. "Just what I thought myself."

She cleared her throat. "Want some more coffee?"

"If you won't have to make a fresh pot," he agreed. He looked down at his strong wrist. "I have to go by ten-thirty. I'm expecting a phone call."

It was almost ten-fifteen now, she thought miserably. She was disappointed at that, but astonished at what she saw on his wrist. She got up, trying not to appear as uneasy as she felt, and poured coffee into the cups. But her mind wasn't on coffee. It was on the watch he was wearing. She knew a Rolex when she saw one, and she knew what they cost. He couldn't have bought that on a mechanic's salary.

It was almost confirmation of the theory that he had to be on somebody's payroll besides MacFaber's. For one sweet moment she wondered if he might be MacFaber's private detective. They made good money, didn't they?

She turned, watching him watch the mystery movie. Wouldn't a detective like such a program?

She took the coffee back in and sat down beside him. Life was taking on a whole new meaning.

"Do you like mysteries?" she asked during a lull in the action.

"Very much," he confessed. He smiled down at her. "I like solving them, too."

"So do I. I always wanted to be a secret agent."

His dark eyes narrowed. "Really?"

"But I never actually did it, of course," she murmured. "Like everything else in my life, it was just a dream."

He was watching her closely, making lightning adjustments. He had to find out the truth about her. He'd missed her ridiculously while he'd been away. Being with her again was like coming home.

She tried to watch the program, but she was all too aware of how late it was and how little time she was going to have with him. He might even have forgotten that he'd promised to take her bowling on Saturday. He might not want to anymore.

His big hand slid between them, and curled around hers, tightening as the action unfolded on the screen. She wasn't even watching. Her eyes were on his broad face, riveted to its hard strength.

"Why don't you ever answer your damned phone at night?"

She knew she'd gasped. She always unplugged the telephone at nine, so that she could watch television undisturbed and go to bed when she pleased without nuisance calls. Those were the only kind she ever got, now that her parents were dead. It had never occurred to her that Jake might be trying to telephone her.

"I unplug it at nine," she said in soft disbelief.

"I called every night at eleven," he replied. "It was impossible to phone you at work, and I was tied up until the wee hours every night."

"You tried to call me?" she asked, aghast.

"Don't look so surprised," he murmured dryly. "Aren't you even experienced enough to know when a man's interested in you?"

She lowered her eyes. "It can be unpleasant to build sand castles in the surf," she said noncommittally.

"It can be unpleasant to build them anywhere."

His hand, big and warm and gentle, caressed hers. It had a rough feel to it, and that puzzled her. It had been her experience that men's hands were relatively smooth when they were used to building or fixing things. Callused hands usually went with rough sports.

"You have to take chances in this life if you want to accomplish anything," he continued.

"So they say." Her eyes sought his, huge and bright through the lenses of her glasses. "But I'm afraid to take chances."

"Are you really?" he asked, voicing his thoughts out loud. His hand left hers and curled around her nape, tugging her head up so that her mouth could meet the slow, confident descent of his.

She gave in almost immediately. He made sweet surges of pleasure run through her body like fire when he kissed her. It was never the same kiss twice, either. This one was slow and steady and a little rough. It was less expert than his others, almost as if he'd been experimenting before and he was deadly serious now.

"Bagwell . . ." she began.

"Damn Bagwell. Come here." He pulled her across his lap in one easy, smooth motion, his mouth covering hers to still any protests she might make.

His big arms swallowed her, enveloped her. He twisted her so that her stomach was pressing against his, and one enormous hand went to the base of her spine to hold her there when she panicked and tried to pull back.

She'd never felt the full arousal of a man's body before, and it embarrassed her. But trying to struggle embarrassed her more, because his body made an emphatic statement about what her movements did to it, and against her lips, he groaned harshly.

With a faint sigh, she gave in. She didn't want to hurt him. Besides all that, she thought bitterly, she might never be held like this again. And she was beginning to care very much about this big, quiet man.

She pressed one slender hand flat against his shirt front, fascinated by the sheer breadth of his chest and the cushy warmth of it under the thin knit fabric.

His heartbeat increased at the unconscious motion of her fingers. "Unbutton it," he said against her mouth.

She felt an explosion of sensation. Did he mean it? Was he giving her free license to explore him, to touch him? She'd never wanted to touch a man under his shirt before. But then, Jake was no ordinary man.

She lay against him, feeling his body throb while she debated whether or not it would be sane to do as he asked. But she was awash in new pleasures, enjoying the scent of his cologne, the hard beat of his heart under her hand, the feel of his big body all around her in a feverishly close intimacy. She looked up into stormy black eyes in a face like stone, and she didn't even hesitate.

Her unsteady fingers went to the top three buttons and she unfastened them one by one, disclosing a darkly tanned chest thick with black, curling hair. She hesitated, her eyes mirroring her uncertainty as she looked up at him.

"Don't stop there," he said quietly. "I can't think of anything I'd enjoy more than feeling your hands on me."

Five

────

Maureen looked up at Jake with her heart in her eyes. He'd been kind to her, and she felt like a woman when he kissed her. But he was rushing her into an intimacy that she wasn't certain she was ready for. She was a slow starter. She needed time.

He felt her hesitation. His big hand touched hers where it paused at the fourth button of his shirt. "I'm not asking you to give yourself to me," he said quietly. "I want you to touch me. But not unless you want it, too."

That relaxed her tightly strung nerves. She lay against him, burying her face against his hair-roughened skin where the fabric of his shirt was open, feeling him go taut. "I can't go to bed with you," she said in a hesitant whisper.

He stroked her hair gently. "You will, eventually," he said. "But we'll go slow. Come up here and kiss me. I've got to go in five minutes."

"How unflattering," she managed with a nervous laugh, glancing up. "You can keep up with the time—"

"I have to. I'm a businessman first and foremost," he murmured dryly. He bent and put his mouth over hers, holding the faint pressure until the kiss broke through her reserves and forced her to link her arms around his neck, pushing upward to coax his mouth closer.

"Is this what you want?" he asked huskily, and his hand went behind her head. The kiss was long and slow and terribly arousing. He didn't try to undress her, or even touch her intimately. The most intimate thing he did was to smooth her hand against his chest and press it hard over his heart while his mouth worked against hers with increasing ardor. The controlled ferocity of the kiss made her body writhe against his, and that was when he suddenly put her away and got to his feet.

She lay there with Bagwell fluffed up and half-asleep at the foot of the sofa, watching Jake move away to light a cigarette with his back to her.

"I have to go," he said shortly.

Oh, Lord, she thought, I've done it now. He'll go away and never come back....

He turned then, and she saw his broad face dark with frustrated passion, hard with desire. And she knew without being told that he wasn't going to go away. If she was enthralled, so was he. He might not like it, but he was as helpless as she was. The chemistry between them was too sweet to ignore.

She was suddenly glad that he was a mechanic, and not some rich man with designs on her virtue. At least, even if he turned out to be on Peters's payroll, he was just an ordinary man. She could live with an avaricious streak, she told herself. She could live with anything, rather than lose Jake.

"Deep thoughts, Maureen?" he asked quietly.

"I'm glad you're just a mechanic," she said softly. "Just an ordinary man. I like what you are."

His face went harder. "Maybe I'm not what I seem to be," he said, because her ardor had shaken him.

She wondered then if she'd been right all along, and he really was a saboteur. But it didn't seem to matter. "I don't care what you are," she replied recklessly. "It doesn't matter."

"You might find that it could matter a great deal," he told her, his dark eyes stormier than ever. He checked his watch and cursed under his breath. "I've got to go. I'll see you at work tomorrow."

"All right." She got up, her legs wobbly, her hair wild, her lips faintly swollen but still hungry for his.

He caught her hand in his and walked with her to the door, pausing to reach down and press a long, smoky kiss against her open mouth.

"You're sweet to kiss," he whispered. He nipped her lower lip ardently. "Get some sleep. Good night."

"Good night."

He was gone before she could say another word. She put Bagwell to bed, much later than she should have, covered him and went to her own bed. But she didn't sleep. On the other side of the wall, she could hear Jake's deep, slow voice. She couldn't make out what he was saying, but he sounded angry and the conversation went on for a long time. She was still hearing it drifting in and out when she finally went to sleep, worried to death about Jake's future. Somehow she had to protect him from MacFaber, if Jake really was a saboteur. She didn't know how she was going to do it, but she'd manage something. She had to. She couldn't let anything happen to him.

The next morning, everything seemed to be upside down at work. Mr. Blake, who was never late, wasn't at his desk. Maureen dealt with the mail as usual and answered the phone, but she couldn't do the reports or answer technical letters. Eventually, she just sat at her desk, waiting, with the feeling of sitting on an unexploded bomb.

When lunchtime came and her boss still hadn't, she began to worry. Her first thought was of Jake. Maybe he'd been found out! Maybe they'd caught him!

She went to the canteen to eat, hoping for a glimpse of him there, but he was nowhere in sight. In desperation, Maureen stopped by MacFaber's office to see if his secretary might know what was going on.

"Is something afoot?" Maureen whispered.

Charlene looked up from the computer screen. "Sure. Twelve inches is a foot." She grinned.

"I hate you."

"So do I sometimes," her friend agreed. "Why the worried look?"

"Mr. Blake isn't in his office."

"I guess not. MacFaber's what's afoot," she whispered confidentially. "He's back in town and out for blood. I hear he's got all the top-level executives on the carpet at a motel outside the city limits, giving them hell."

"Have they caught the culprit?" Maureen asked with commendable restraint.

"What culprit?" Charlene frowned.

"The one who's messed up the Faber jet."

"Oh, that culprit." Charlene grinned. "I think so, but they aren't saying who it is. However, I have it from a confidential source that there's going to be another test flight a week from tomorrow. Then we'll know."

Maureen's heart was going like a watch. "I don't guess they've mentioned any names?"

Charlene shook her head. "Not a chance. And it doesn't sound like sabotage, exactly. All I can tell you is that Mr. Blake went looking for MacFaber last night, from what the grapevine says, and this morning there's a very hush-hush staff meeting." She lowered her voice. "And apparently MacFaber's private detective has done a slick job, hanging around here incognito while he smoked out the cause of the failed test flight. From what I hear, there really was someone at fault. Someone in the mechanical section, and based right here."

Maureen felt sick. Then the part about the private detective being incognito touched her mind. Bells began ringing in Maureen's head. Was it possible that Jake could be MacFaber's private detective? That thought gave her hope. At least there was a chance that he might not be the spy she'd thought he was. And he'd told her that he could be something besides what he seemed. Her gloomy spirits lifted a little.

"Are you okay? You look white."

Maureen snapped herself back to the present. "I'm okay." She smiled wanly, adjusted her glasses and went back to her own office. She sat there until midafternoon, brooding over her mechanic. It wasn't until Mr. Blake came in, pale and exhausted, that she was able to divert her mind.

"I don't want to answer any more questions." He held up his hand when she started to speak. "So just get your pad, please, Maureen, and we'll get to the mail."

He sat down heavily at his desk and Maureen did what she was told, blazing with unanswered questions.

She went home, still without having seen Jake anywhere at all. What if he'd been arrested?

She fixed a meager supper of ham sandwiches, sharing part of it with Bagwell, trying not to cry. Her life was over. She'd never see Jake again. He'd go to prison—

There was a sharp knock at the door. She ran to open it, and there he was. He looked tired and half out of sorts. But to Maureen, he was the most beautiful sight she'd seen all day.

With a hard sob, she threw herself into his arms.

"What's this all about?" he asked at her temple. "What's wrong?"

"Was it you?" she asked, lifting tragic eyes to his. "They had this big meeting, and I couldn't find you. I thought...thought maybe they'd arrested you for sabotage or something!"

He was very still. His hands tightened on her shoulders. "You thought it was me?" he prompted, aghast at her assumption.

"Well, you're new," she groaned. "And they said they thought it was a mechanic, and I didn't know if you were working for Mr. Peters...." She drew back and looked up into his shocked face. "I'm sorry. I'm ashamed that I thought such a thing about you. And I knew, too, that you might be MacFaber's private detective?" Her voice went up, and she watched him, hoping for some reaction. But there was nothing. His features were as calm as if he were watching a weather report on television.

He wondered what she'd say if he admitted that he'd thought it was her. He was certain now, of course, that it wasn't. Or reasonably certain. A week from tomorrow would be the telling day, when the jet flew or didn't. Meanwhile, he didn't dare answer her suspicions one way or the other. At this point it was too risky.

He touched her hair. "You think I'm a saboteur?" he asked with a faint smile, a little cynical about her acceptance of him despite her suspicions. "And you don't mind?"

"You're my friend," she said simply. She grimaced. "Go ahead. Walk out and never come back. It's all I deserve."

He didn't budge. His dark eyes narrowed under his heavy brow. "Why did you keep seeing me?" he asked.

"At first I was keeping you under surveillance," she murmured with a shy grin. "And then..." The smile faded as her eyes searched his. "You aren't in trouble, are you?" she asked huskily. "I'll be a character witness if you need one. I'll do anything I can to help."

"Will you?" He tugged a lock of her hair. "Is this concern real, or have you found out more than just what went wrong with the Faber jet?" he asked from an acquired distrust of women.

She stared at him blankly. "I don't understand."

He sighed. Perhaps she didn't. She might not know who he really was. "Never mind. What are we eating? I'm starved!"

The question, so domestic, made her tingle with pleasure. She didn't make a single remark about his assumption that she was inviting him to eat with her. It was such a joy to have him in her apartment—in her life—that the thought that he might be presumptuous never even occurred to her.

She grinned. "We're having ham sandwiches and Jell-O."

He made a face. "Get something on and I'll take you out for crepes and shortcake."

"It's too late," she said. "And you shouldn't spend your paycheck on me." She felt brave, and because she did, she nestled closely in his arms with a long breath and closed her eyes, inhaling the delicious fragrance of his very masculine cologne. "I'm glad you're not in trouble."

His big hands spread over her back. Odd, to feel so protective about this woman. She wasn't beautiful. She didn't have money. She wasn't sophisticated, and she didn't come from an uptown family. She wasn't even his kind of companion. So why did he feel so comfortable with her?

"Mr. Blake wouldn't tell me anything, and Charlene couldn't," she said against his shirt. "But something's going on, I can feel it. They say that Mr. MacFaber's private detective struck pay dirt."

"So I've heard."

"Good for him. Poor old Mr. MacFaber..."

"What makes you think he's old?" he asked dryly.

"Oh, Charlene says he's forty at least," she murmured. "And overweight and graying. I guess he's worn out his body with South American heiresses and solitary sports."

He chuckled. "Maybe he has. I wouldn't put too much stock in the South American heiress, though. I don't think MacFaber is much of a ladies' man. From what I hear, he isn't at all the type."

"Really?" She lifted her head and looked up at him. "That will break hearts around the office." She laughed softly. "All the girls are waiting with bated breath for him to make an appearance. His publicity has preceded him, you see. Everyone thinks he's Mr. Right. Even two of the engaged girls! There'll be a scandal when he shows up."

"I wouldn't doubt it." He let her go and moved away. "Hello, Bagwell."

The big parrot spared him a disinterested glance and went back to nibbling on the bread and ham in his claw.

"How many can you eat?" Maureen asked, unwrapping bread.

"If you mean parrots, I'm not sure," he said. "Are you offering me Bagwell in a cheese sauce?"

"Not parrots—" she laughed gaily "—sandwiches. Ham. With cheese and lettuce and mayonnaise."

"And mustard," he instructed. "Two."

"Okay."

She made them, delighted to see him, to have him sitting so naturally at her kitchen table. While she made sandwiches, he pulled off his jacket and tie and tossed them over an empty chair out of Bagwell's reach. He crossed his long legs and unbuttoned the throat of his white shirt. This was an expensive shirt, too, she noticed as she finished making sandwiches and opened a bag of potato chips to go with them. It looked very much like silk. She wondered where he'd been that he'd had to dress up, but she didn't pry.

"I like this," he murmured, nodding when she offered to pour him a cup of coffee. "I can't remember the last time a woman made me supper."

"I'll bet your mother did."

His eyes narrowed suddenly and he watched her warily. "What do you know about my mother?"

"Well, what could I know, since I've only just met you?" she asked reasonably. "But my mother used to make things for me, so I assume yours did for you."

"Of course." He lifted the black coffee to his chiseled mouth. "My mother couldn't cook. She was completely undomesticated."

"Do you have brothers and sisters?"

He shook his head. "I have no one. Not anymore."

"I'm sorry."

"Why? You don't have anyone, either."

"That's true." She sat down across from him and offered Bagwell another piece of sandwich and then wolfed down her own. She was aware of the too-tight T-shirt she was wearing with her worn jeans. But her guest didn't seem to notice or mind, except that his dark eyes lingered just a little too long for politeness on the thrust of her breasts—especially when that scrutiny made the tips very obvious.

"Why did you tie up your hair that way?" he asked, nodding toward her ponytail. "It doesn't suit you at all."

"Thanks a lot!"

"I like it long." He took another bite out of his sandwich and chewed carefully before he swallowed it down with a sip of coffee. His dark eyes met hers and he smiled amusedly. "Take that ponytail down and I might make love to you."

Her heart leaped. "No," she said with faint humor. "You don't have sex with virgins. You said so."

"Make love," he whispered, his dark eyes holding her green ones as he smiled. "Not have sex."

She colored but her gaze didn't waver. "What's the difference?"

"Only an innocent could ask a question like that." He finished his second sandwich and leaned back to sip his coffee. "Those were good."

"Thank you," she said, wondering how a man could mix sex with ham sandwiches in the same conversation.

He nibbled on a potato chip while he studied her. "How was your boss today?" he asked out of the blue.

"Mr. Blake?" she asked absently, offering Bagwell a potato chip. "He was rather preoccupied. I wanted to ask him what he'd found out about the saboteur, but he wasn't talking. I think Mr. MacFaber had made mincemeat out of him," she said with a smile. "Charlene said he was giving the executives hell."

"Which they richly deserved," he returned. His eyes went hard as he sipped his coffee. "The whole damned project could have been scrapped over one man's stupid mistake.''

Her eyebrows arched. ''What do you know about it?''

''Mechanics know everything,'' he said easily.

''Oh.'' She got up and poured some more coffee. ''You look tired.''

''I feel tired.'' He leaned back and closed his eyes with a sigh. ''I'm getting too old for my life-style, did you know, Maureen? I think I'm going to have to slow down.''

''Nonsense. You're only as old as you think you are.'' She touched his thick, black hair hesitantly. ''You ought to go home and go to bed,'' she said gently.

His hand caught hers and his eyes opened, looking up into hers. ''Sleep with me.''

She flushed. ''No.''

''Just sleep,'' he murmured with a soft smile. ''I'm too tired for anything else.''

''That wouldn't be a good idea,'' she said, hating her inhibitions, because she'd never wanted anything more than to curl up beside him in a bed and feel him holding her close in the darkness. But it would be too dangerous.

''Why not?'' he persisted.

''Because something could happen.'' Her eyes darted to his and away again. ''Jake, I don't even know how to take precautions.''

He frowned as he studied her downcast face. She was a throwback to another age. And yet, there was something so vulnerable about her, so deeply loving. He wondered how it would be if she loved him. He wondered how it would be if she was carrying his child.

His own thought irritated him. He let go of her hand. ''You're right. Something could happen, and it's too soon.'' He got to his feet, stretching lazily. ''I'm sorry I couldn't make our bowling date,'' he said suddenly. ''So how about tomorrow night? We'll have Chinese food and bowl afterward.''

She felt her heart leap. "Tomorrow night?"

"Yes."

Her face brightened. "I'd love to."

"I'll pick you up at six." He curved his hand over Bagwell's sleepy head and ruffled it affectionately. "He's getting used to me."

"It does seem that way." She smiled.

He glanced down at her. "Are you getting used to me, too?"

"I'm afraid so," she said, her voice husky with feeling.

He moved toward her, his big hands catching her waist and pulling her gently against him in a nonthreatening way. "Don't brood about things at work," he said, bending his head. "Everything's going to be all right. Kiss me."

She did, loving the feel of his hard mouth moving against hers, because she'd been aching for this ever since he'd walked in the door. But if she hoped for violent ardor, she was disappointed. It was a brief kiss and very chaste. He drew back immediately, leaving her bereft. She wanted him to kiss her as hungrily as he had the last time he'd been in her apartment. She wanted him to touch her, to look at her. But he smiled gently and put her away from him. It took all her willpower not to beg him to kiss her again. But he released her with a warm smile and moved away. "I hope you like Chinese food," he remarked as he moved to the door.

"I love it," she said breathlessly. She did, but she'd have loved cultivated alfalfa in wine sauce if it meant eating in Jake's company.

"Good." He studied her quietly. She looked frustrated, all right, as if she'd wanted far more than that teasing kiss. So had he, but it was the wrong time for what it might lead to. She wasn't ready for any kind of commitment. In fact, neither was he. And the thought of turning her helpless longing for him into a one-night stand was distasteful. He wanted her, but the thought of seducing her disturbed him, made him ashamed of even considering something so underhanded with a woman like Maureen.

He didn't really understand the effect she had on him. She wasn't pretty. She was really rather shy under her bubbly exterior. She didn't know how to kiss and she'd probably faint if he tried to undress her. His heart began to beat heavily at that thought. She was virginal, and all her responses to him would be new ones; all her repressed hungers would find their satisfaction in him. It made him faintly dizzy just to consider the pleasure of initiating her. He opened the door, hoping that the cool night air would bring him to his senses. They were worlds apart. He couldn't afford to seduce her. She was the kind of woman who equated sex with a wedding ring, and he didn't want to get married. He didn't have room in his life for a woman full-time.

"Lock the door behind me," he said, because he felt protective all the same.

"I will. Good night," she said, her voice soft. But he went out without another word, solemn and quiet.

She felt solemn herself when he'd gone. She didn't know what to do. She had an insane urge to run. He was going to seduce her. She knew it, and she wasn't sure how she was going to live with herself. She wanted him desperately. Incredible—to be her age and so stupid about men.

She got into her pajama top and climbed into bed, but all she did was toss and turn, long after Bagwell had sung himself to sleep.

Finally, in desperation, she got up and went into the kitchen to make herself a cup of hot chocolate. But even after she'd swallowed it down, she was still restless and nervous. She went to bed at last, exhausted, and fell asleep almost at once.

But her mind was working even in her sleep, dreaming about Jake. In her dreams, he was undressing her, very slowly, as he kissed her. She felt the impact of his eyes on her body, looking at places she'd never let any other man see, putting his mouth on her so hungrily that even now she could feel the warm moistness over her breast.

She groaned in her sleep.

The dreams were so vivid that she could feel his big hands on her body, gently probing. He touched her ardently as his tongue went into her mouth and she stiffened at the power of a surge of pleasure so sweeping that she cried out loudly. The sound shocked her awake and she sat up in bed, drenched with sweat and trembling from the fever the erotic dream had kindled in her.

She got up, shaking a little as she went into the kitchen and looked at the clock. It was only five, but she knew that she'd never get back to sleep again. She'd forgotten her glasses and she couldn't even see to make coffee without them, but when she started back toward the bedroom, a sharp knock on the door halted her in her tracks.

She paused at the door, hesitating. "Who is it?" she called in a high, nervous voice.

"Oh, for God's sake, who does it sound like?" came a deep snarl from the other side of the wooden door.

She fumbled the chain off, forgetting that she was wearing nothing except the long, sexy pajama top, and opened the door.

If she was underdressed, so was he. Despite her lack of glasses, she could see him very well because he was barely a foot away when he stepped into the kitchen and shut the door behind him. She stood there staring helplessly, unable to speak or even move.

He was wearing light slacks, nothing else. He was barefoot, and there were acres of broad, bare chest in front of her. He was very dark, and powerfully built, with bronze skin and thick hair that ran from his collarbone down his broad chest to his narrow waist and into the belt of his slacks. His arms were muscular. He was built like a professional wrestler and she knew that she was gaping, but she didn't even care. He was delicious.

He noticed the blank stare and attributed it to the fact that she wasn't wearing her glasses. He knew how nearsighted she was. He sighed heavily. "Well?" he asked shortly.

"Well, what?" she mumbled, disoriented.

"I heard you cry out."

She went beet red as she stared up into a broad, hard face with bloodshot eyes that were faintly hostile. "I, uh, was dreaming," she faltered.

He noted the blush. "It must have been some dream."

The blush got worse. "It was." She dropped her eyes to his chest, but that only made matters worse. She wanted to get close to him and jerk open her pajama top and rub her skin against his. The unfamiliar thought shocked her.

"I thought you were having a nightmare," he murmured, watching her. "But passion and fear sound very much alike, don't they?"

"I don't know much about passion...."

He moved closer so that he was right up against her, his big hands warm and caressing on her upper arms. Her breath sighed out against his chest and she wanted so badly to lay her head against him and push close, so that her breasts would flatten against the hard muscle of his stomach....

"Tell me about the dream," he said at her forehead. His lips smoothed over her temple and down to her closed eyelids, her nose, her cheeks. "Tell me why you cried out."

"You . . . you were . . . touching me," she choked, beyond lying as his hands moved down to her waist and pulled her gently against him.

His heart began to beat heavily. His fingers splayed, feeling the softness of her skin under the thin fabric. "Touching you where?" he whispered.

She pressed her face against his chest, savoring the thick wiriness of his chest hair, the scent of his body. "I can't . . . !"

"You smell of roses, Maureen." His hands hesitated, and then moved slowly lower, to find her hips and pull them very gently against his.

She gasped as she felt his aroused body and she tried to move back, but his hands were gently firm.

"This, for a man, signals his vulnerability to a woman," he said at her forehead. "It's not so much a statement of masculine capability as it is a sign of helpless attraction. So why does it frighten you to feel me this way?"

"I've never . . . felt any other man this way," she replied, stiffening a little.

"Not even in that hot little dream you just had?" he whispered huskily.

Her eyes closed tightly. "I've never had a dream like that before," she confessed.

"I heard you through the bedroom wall," he whispered. "You cried out." His hands gently lifted her hips into an even more intimate embrace and he felt her body tremble. "I can bring those sounds out of you again, for real. I can make you feel the pleasure you felt in the dream, with my hands and my mouth."

She shivered with the remembered pleasure of the dream. Her nails bit into his big, warm arms. "It's too soon," she managed, even though her body was in torment to know his touch.

"Are you sure?"

She swallowed and gritted her teeth. Her legs were trembling against his, and he could surely feel it. "I'm sure," she choked.

He let her put a fraction of an inch of space between them, and his hands slid up to her waist. He was breathing unsteadily, and she thought she could hear his heartbeat.

"No, you aren't," he mused, smiling. "But I'll let you off the hook this time." He looked down at her pajama top, where the outline of her breasts pushed against the fabric. "Even though I know how badly you want me to touch you."

Her eyes met his shyly. "How...do you know?" she whispered through her faint embarrassment.

"By this," he whispered back, and holding her eyes, he rubbed his thumb gently over a hard nipple, feeling her body jerk as she gasped in unexpected pleasure. "Feel it?" he asked gently. "Is this what I did to you in your dreams?"

"You...you took off my shirt..." she said on a shuddering breath. Her green eyes were enormous and misty, dazed with sensation as his thumb moved again.

"Like this?" he asked in a slow, normal tone, and his fingers slowly eased the big buttons out of their buttonholes until she was standing vulnerable in front of him, with the jacket on the floor and her soft, pink breasts only a little paler than the pink silk briefs she was wearing under the pajama top.

Six

The impact of his eyes on her body was shattering. Her cheeks were blazing with heat at her own wantonness in letting him see her this way, and her hands trembled as they tried to push at his hair-roughened chest so that she could retrieve her top.

But he pulled her, so gently, against his big, warm body, and made her watch as her taut breasts vanished into the thick pelt of hair over his hard muscles.

"I can hold you like this all morning without losing my head," he said quietly, watching her face, "so don't panic and start fighting for your honor. I know you don't want raw sex and I'm not offering it to you. Put your arms around me. I want to feel the softness of your breasts against me for a few minutes, and then I'll go."

She colored at the sophisticated statement. He made her feel utterly green, which, of course, she was. She slid her arms shakily around him and pressed close, as she'd longed to do for so many lonely nights. She moaned softly at the exquisite sensation of skin on skin, of his arms holding her, of the faintly abrasive and sensual hair of his chest and flat stomach against her bare breasts. She shuddered as she laid her cheek against him.

"Another first?" he asked over her head, and she managed to nod. He moved her lazily against him, laughing softly with pure delight at the way she gasped, at the feel of her body.

"Jake!" she cried out, shaking.

His hands slid from her waist to just under her arms, his thumbs sliding softly against the swell of her breasts. "We'll stop in a minute," he said reassuringly. "Don't faint...."

As he spoke, his hands moved, and they were suddenly on her, swallowing her as his head bent. "Lift up to me, baby," he whispered, his mouth open. He felt her shaky, helpless movement, and then he had her under his mouth, in his mouth, enjoying her silky skin with feverish pleasure. He felt her shiver at the faint suction he created, and his big hands lifted her into the aroused contours of his body as he enjoyed her for minutes that stretched on erotically.

But his resolution not to let things get out of hand was becoming shakier by the minute. She was making noises that made him stiffen with need. Her hands were in his thick dark hair, pulling his mouth even closer against her breasts, and she was moving rhythmically, in time with the caresses of his mouth—until, finally, his need became too urgent to ignore. He'd promised her that he could do this and not lose his head. In fact he had, a dozen times in his youth. But this was different. This was like no other time for him, and he knew that it was going to be agony to stop at all.

He lifted his head to look at a face he didn't even recognize. Her head was thrown back, her long hair spilling almost to her waist in a glorious dark tangle, her eyes slitted with pleasure, her face flushed, her mouth swollen and vulnerable.

His own eyes were black with desire, and his hands had a faint tremor as they held her waist firmly. "I need you," he said huskily. "And you need me. Let me take you to bed."

"I could get pregnant, Jake," she whispered fearfully. Her need for him was no lie, but years of conditioning made her panic and she pushed at his hard chest. "Let me go! Please, I can't . . . !"

"Stand still, for God's sake!" he groaned, shuddering from her unknowing provocation. He held her firmly, stilling her movements, and stood shivering, with his head bowed, trying to breathe, trying to stop the raging urgency from bending him double with frustrated pain.

"I'm sorry," she faltered inadequately.

He shuddered again. His head lifted and his eyes held hers relentlessly. "I can prevent a child," he said roughly. "I've got something in my wallet."

She wanted to. She wanted him. But there were barriers in her mind, put there by her strict upbringing, kept there by her own beliefs and values. He didn't want commitment, she knew that, and she couldn't go to bed with him without it. A one-night stand was the last thing in the world she wanted, even with Jake.

Her stubborn hesitation made him angry. He breathed deliberately, but he was hurting. He glared at her through a red rage. "Setting traps?" he asked in a softly contemptuous tone. "You're going to hold out for a wedding ring, is that how it goes?" He smiled with cold cynicism and pushed her away none too gently. He reached down to swipe up her pajama top and fling it at her. "Well, don't hold your breath, honey. That's been tried, too. I've never wanted any woman enough to sacrifice my freedom for a few minutes of feverish coupling in a bed."

He made it sound cheap and sordid. She closed her eyes and shivered now with distaste as she got back into her pajama top and buttoned it with trembling fingers. She was glad she wasn't wearing her glasses. She couldn't bear the contempt in his eyes. But he'd gotten it all wrong. She wasn't trying to tease or blackmail him into marriage. She'd been as far gone as he had. It was just that she had too many scruples to give herself without love on both sides.

He felt furious. Her shoulders were slumped with defeat and she looked as if he'd slapped her. He ground his teeth at what he'd said and done. He should never have let things go so far. He'd even promised her that he could control their lovemaking, and look what had happened. But the sight of her in that pajama top had made him blind with passion. Just the smell of her, the scent of roses that clung to her, aroused him.

"I have to get dressed," she said in a husky, shamed tone. She turned and went into the bedroom and closed the door, leaning against it with tears streaming down her cheeks. She never wanted to see him again. She hadn't thought that anything could hurt so much. He'd been so gentle with her, so loving, and then to say—that! He only wanted her body, not her mind and heart. He was a man on the make!

"Maureen."

She sniffed back the tears and locked the bedroom door with an audible click. She didn't answer him, because she didn't want him to hear how upset she was.

He knew already. He'd heard the sniffing. He sighed heavily and leaned his forehead against the door. "I'll see you tonight," he said. "I have to go."

She managed to control the quaver in her voice. "I won't go out with you tonight, Jake," she said proudly. "Thanks all . . . all the same. Goodbye."

He paused, bristling with anger and frustration and bad temper. He moved away from the bedroom door with fury in his dark eyes. "If that's how you want it, it's fine with me. I must have better things to do with my spare time than carting around a stone virgin!"

She closed her eyes as his angry footsteps faded away. A door slammed. She leaned back against the bedroom door, letting the tears fall. Well, she knew now what he really thought of her. It was her own fault, anyway; she should never have let him touch her. Now he was gone and she'd never see him again. She hated herself. She hated him even more.

She dressed, trying not to look at her chastened face in the mirror as she put her hair into a tight bun and smeared on a minimum of makeup to go with her simple blue knit dress. She made breakfast and fed Bagwell, and went to work with her heart around her knees.

Jake was nowhere in sight that day, and he didn't come home that night. She'd glanced helplessly out the back door to see if his truck was in the driveway, but it wasn't. Well, she thought miserably, what had she expected? She'd sent him running. She must have some kind of knack for keeping attractive men at bay, because she'd done a magnificent job with Jake.

Saturday came, finally, and at least it was a clear, sunny day so that she could get out in the backyard with her hoe and weed her small vegetable patch. But her heart wasn't really in it. She felt guilty that she'd let Jake touch her the

way he had. It had probably sent him off the deep end and
led to their almost violent confrontation. If she'd called a
halt at once, they'd still be friends. But she'd loved what
he'd been doing to her.

With a heavy sigh, she wielded her hoe. Her hair was
pulled into a bun. She wore no makeup at all. With her
jeans and sandals she wore an old, oversize cotton shirt,
the back of which bore a logo marking 150 years of inde-
pendence for Texas. She looked young and vulnerable, but
not at all sexy—which was what she'd wanted. She had to
learn to control those wanton feelings, she told herself.
Then, maybe the next time—if there was a next time—she
wouldn't land herself in such a miserable emotional mess.
She'd acted like a sophisticated woman, and she wasn't.

She was so wrapped up in her anguish that she didn't
hear Jake until he was standing beside her. Her heart raced
but she couldn't look up at him. She was too ashamed.

His dark eyes slid over her white face with some guilt of
his own. He knew without being told why she was dressed
this way, looking this way. With her strict upbringing,
what he'd done to her would probably have seemed like a
cardinal sin. He hadn't slept a full night since it happened, despite the business that had kept him away from
her. He had regrets of his own, not only about backing her
into a corner as he had, but mostly about the things he'd
said to her.

"Are we still speaking?" he asked with forced careless-
ness. "Or do I have to eat my own cooking again tonight?"

She was staring at her dusty toes in the brown sandals,
feeling very young and nervous. "I didn't think you'd ever
speak to me again," she said quietly. Her lower lip trembled and she caught it in her teeth. "I'm so sorry, Jake!"

He swore softly under his breath and suddenly jerked
her against him, wrapping her up hungrily in his big arms.
He'd never felt so protective about a woman. He hated
seeing her cry and feeling that he was responsible for her
tears. His big arms contracted, pressing her against him.

"I've missed you," he ground out at her temple. He
buried his face in her neck and kissed it ardently, his lean
hands smoothing up and down her back. "My God, I'm
sorry, too! I didn't mean what I said to you that morning."

Her heart lifted magically. He had to care a little, because he'd come back. Her eyes closed and she sighed as
she snuggled closer. At least he didn't hate her anymore.

"It was my fault, too," she said. "I should never
have...have behaved that way with you. I acted like a
streetwalker!"

"No!" He tilted her face up to his, shocked at her incredible statement. "My God, you did nothing of the
sort!"

"I let you look at me like that," she lowered her eyes
and flushed furiously.

He had to catch his breath. He'd never had to deal with
this kind of emotional trauma. The women in his world
were so sophisticated that he couldn't conceive of any of
them being ashamed to let a man see them nude. But, then,
he'd never met anyone like Maureen.

"Did none of your people ever talk to you about sex?"
he asked gently.

She closed her eyes. "Sex before marriage is wrong,"
she whispered. "My parents were very religious people,
Jake, and I am, too." She looked up. "I won't apologize
for my beliefs. I shouldn't have to defend them."

He smiled gently. "No, and I'm not asking you to." He
sighed, touching her face with just his fingertips. "But the

feelings you had when I touched you are very natural. They're part of being a woman. If you couldn't enjoy a man's mouth on yours, a man's hands on your body, you'd only be half alive." He smoothed his hands over her back. "Sex is the basis of our whole species, little one. Without it, you and I wouldn't even be here."

It was hard for her to talk about it. Her eyes lowered to his shirt. It was blue with an emblem on the pocket, and she liked the way it clung to his broad, hard chest, outlining the ripple of muscle when his arms moved closer around her. "I didn't know that it made people so helpless," she confessed shyly.

"Or so hot?" He grinned wickedly.

She smiled at him. "That, too."

"All you have to remember is that men are made in such a way that they're easily aroused and not so easily cooled down. I thought I could look at you without going nuts, and I found out that I couldn't." He nuzzled his nose against hers. "For the first time in my life, I couldn't turn it off when I wanted to," he whispered. "You had me so aroused, I thought I was going to be sick."

Her eyes widened, fascinated.

His lips curved into an amused smile. "You don't understand?" he asked gently. "Then let me explain it to you."

He did, to her shocked embarrassment, so that her face was on fire by the time he finished and she knew her knees were going to collapse under her. No one had ever spoken to her so frankly of intimate things before.

"My gosh!" she burst out, trying to move away from him.

He held her there with controlled gentleness. "That will educate you a little more," he said unashamedly, his dark eyes holding hers without the sparkle of humor they'd had only seconds before. "You'll need to know, because I'm not going away again. It hurts too much to be away from you. Since you don't want an affair with me, we'll have to do things your way. And if you don't tempt me again by walking around in that damned pajama top, we'll get along fine."

"Was that why?" she asked, her voice breathless.

He nodded. "I'd had some dreams of my own about you," he said quietly. "And if you want to know, it takes a lot to arouse me these days. You can do it by walking across a room."

She lowered her eyes quickly. "It might be better if you found someone who didn't have all my hang-ups," she said.

"I don't want someone without your hang-ups." He sighed. "I just want you. In any way you feel comfortable with me. I guess I can live on cold showers and hot dreams if I have to," he said with a rueful smile. "As long as you'll kiss me now and again."

"You make me feel guilty," she said miserably.

"That isn't what I want at all." He bent and brushed his mouth gently against hers, feeling and loving its instant response. "I think I can handle it now without going off the deep end like I did last time," he bit off against her lips. "So open your mouth and let me show you how much I've missed you."

The slow, expert penetration of his tongue made her tense with the kind of fiery desire he'd kindled in her the morning they'd argued. She gasped under his hard lips and felt his hands gathering her roughly to his hips, showing her what he'd explained to her minutes before.

His eyes opened and his mouth lifted slowly, but his hands didn't release her. "Relax," he whispered. "I'm not going to hurt you."

"It embarrasses me," she moaned.

"Only because you're such a sheltered little thing," he breathed. He kissed her eyelids shut and nuzzled his face against hers. "Humor me. This is the most innocent time I've spent with a woman since I became an adult, and I don't think I've ever felt such tenderness. Don't spoil it for me."

She had to fight down the urge to run. Slowly her tense legs gave way and she let him have her weight, surprised to find how easily she fitted against him, how fluid her body could be as he smoothed it intimately against his. His legs trembled faintly, but his hands relaxed their firm grip and became gentle and caressing on her hips.

"Heaven," he whispered. "It's sheer heaven."

Her hands flattened against his chest and she rested her forehead against him with a long, sweet sigh. Yes, it was. The feel of him was no longer frightening, because he wasn't demanding anything. It began to be natural, some-how, as if he belonged to her and always had.

"I guess this is familiar territory for you," she said quietly.

"In some ways." He kissed her forehead with breathless tenderness. "Would you like to know how long it's been since I've had a woman intimately?"

She flushed. "No!"

He smiled against her skin. "It's been two years, Maureen."

That surprised her into lifting her shocked face. He wasn't kidding. It was in his dark eyes, in the hard lines of his face. "Really?" she asked.

He nodded. "I've been busy. Women had begun to lose their appeal for reasons I'll tell you one day. I got tired of being used."

She frowned slightly. "Why would women want to use you?"

He couldn't tell her that. He brushed his mouth gently over hers. "You're very soft," he murmured. "I remember the way you felt against me in your apartment that morning, without your top...."

She buried her face against his chest. "Don't."

His open mouth brushed over her cheek. "The softness in my hands...," he groaned, searching for her mouth again.

She felt the kiss like a brand on her mouth. His body grew even more taut as he deepened the kiss, and his hands slid lower down her body to lift her into shockingly close contact. She'd never felt anything half so intimate. It was like touching a live wire. She cried out and her nails bit into him as he pulled her rhythmically into the changed contours of his big body.

He shuddered suddenly and jerked away from her. He walked off a little way and lit a cigarette with unsteady fingers. In the back of his mind was some crazy song about a family man, and the whole while he'd been holding Maureen, he'd been hearing lullabies. Surely he was going crazy. Missing her had become acutely painful. He'd wanted to stay away, to avoid any more involvement with her. She wouldn't fit into his life, he kept telling himself, and she couldn't give him an affair. But he was helpless. He wanted her too much to walk away. And if her headlong response was any indication, she wanted him every bit as much.

"What are we going to do, Maureen?" he asked, still with his back to her and grateful that the duplex was so secluded that he could kiss her in the yard without any danger of their being seen.

"I don't know," she said, her voice shaking. She wrapped her arms around her aching breasts and stared down at the disturbed earth where she'd been hoeing. "It isn't fair to you!"

He turned then, his face a little paler than it had been, and moved back to her with the smoking cigarette in one big hand. "I'm afraid of marriage," he said gently. "My parents spent twenty years together, and few of them were happy. They always said they'd been in love at the beginning, but they weren't at the end." His big shoulders rose and fell. "I don't know that I could adjust to another person in my life. Or more than one." His dark eyes met hers. "On the other hand, I'd like very much to make you pregnant," he said huskily. "And that scares the hell out of me, do you know that?"

She felt her body tremble as the import of the words sank in. He didn't sound like a man who wanted a quick affair. He sounded like a man with commitment on his mind.

"Are you shocked?" he asked with a faint smile. "So am I. I've never said that to a woman in my life."

She looked up at him with her heart in her eyes. "I'm glad," she whispered.

He sighed, feeling velvet webs spinning around him. It was inevitable, he supposed. He touched her dark hair in its tight bun. "How about putting up that hoe and getting into something dressy?" he asked. "We'll fly down to Galveston and get some seafood."

She laughed. "You crazy man," she said, snuggling against him. "And I suppose you could fly us there in your own airplane and we could go out on your yacht and fish for the seafood ourselves?" She didn't see his face, which had gone white. She laughed again and hugged him. "I like your sense of humor. But I'll be very happy with Long

John Silver's fish and chips. You can sit and talk to Bagwell while I get dressed."

She moved away and he followed her, scowling. This
was going to be more complicated than he'd imagined.
After that test flight on Friday, he wouldn't be able to keep
secrets from her. Everything would be made public, in-
cluding his identity. He cursed under his breath. If only
she'd been a liberated, sophisticated woman, he could have
taken her to bed and worked her out of his system. But she
was the kind of woman he'd dreamed of all his life, and he
wanted things with her and of her that he'd never wanted
before. It was going to lead to tragedy in the end, if he
couldn't level with her in time.

He took her to one of those fast-food places and they ate
fish while he glanced around him with interest. He'd
known of places like this, of course, but they weren't usually part of his life-style. His dark eyes lingered on the ordinary people sitting in small groups. Men in suits, women
in knit pantsuits, teenagers in skimpy summer clothing.
Some of the older men and women wore their life stories
in the wrinkles and lines on their faces. There were labor-
ers and farmers and seamstresses; secretaries and young
executives. He stared at them and felt suddenly as if he'd
missed the boat. He'd lived dangerously, and he'd lived
well. But these people knew life as he never really had.

"Deep thoughts?" she asked gently.

"Very deep." He sipped his black coffee. "Do you come
here often?" he asked and was genuinely curious.

"About once a week. Some days it's chili, others it's
hamburgers—on the weekends, I mean. I eat in the canteen or take my lunch at work. I try to be punctual," she
said with a smile. "I think we need to give a day's work for
a day's pay, however out of style that sounds."

He smiled. "Oh, I approve wholeheartedly," he murmured. "And I'm certain MacFaber would agree."

"Poor old thing," she said, her eyes softening. "He must be very alone. He has no family, you know, and his mother died last year."

He lowered his dark eyes to his coffee. "He's filthy rich. I imagine he can buy love."

"Not the real thing. Only an expensive imitation of it." She slid her hand to Jake's and touched it lightly, hesitantly. Her eyes met his dark ones and she shivered at the intensity in them. "I never knew what love was...before," she said.

He didn't hear the buzz of conversation around them. He only heard her voice, saw her face. His head spun at what she was admitting to him. His fingers slid around hers and contracted hungrily, and she smiled at him with eyes that worshiped him. He felt like getting on the table and dancing, but he only smiled back at her.

Those were words he'd never said and meant. It surprised him that he could almost have said them to her with genuine feeling. But he kept his silence. He had a foreboding about Friday. He had to find a way to tell her before then.

After they ate, they went to a matinee, walked around the shopping mall twice, and finally wound up at the bowling alley. But all the lanes were full, so they sat and drank coffee and watched.

He took her home late, pausing at her doorway to kiss her hungrily and hard.

"No, I won't come inside with you," he whispered, touching his finger to her lips. "It's too risky."

She looked at him worriedly. "Jake, I might be able..."

"It would be like raping you, don't you understand?" he asked with soft fervor. "Unless you felt right about it,

I might as well force you. And I could never do that. Now go to bed. I'll come for you in the morning and we'll go to church. Okay?"

She smiled. "Okay."

He touched the tip of her nose, winked, and walked away whistling.

The next few days were magic. They went everywhere together except at work, and she never seemed to see him there anymore. She asked him about it on Thursday afternoon when she got home from the office. He was in the yard, waiting, when she drove up.

"Aren't you at the plant these days?" she asked as she got out of the car.

He grinned. "I'm on vacation, didn't you know?" He kissed her softly. "And no, I'm not the culprit they caught messing around with MacFaber's jet, in case you were still wondering about me."

She shook her head. "Oh, no," she said softly. "I knew that days ago. I'm not sure how I knew, I just did." Her eyes adored him. "I don't care who you are, or what you do."

That was obvious and it made him feel ten feet tall. At the same time, it made him feel guilty as hell. He'd learned a lot about her. The most important thing he'd learned was that she didn't have a mercenary bone in her body.

He glanced at the sweat on her forehead and the glare of the sun. "Want to lie out and sunbathe with me for a few minutes?" he asked. "It's still hours until dark, but late enough so that we won't get burned."

She smiled gaily. "I'd love it. I have a bikini I've never worn." She colored. "It's a little too risqué for my taste...." Her smile faded. "On second thought, maybe I shouldn't wear it?"

He cocked an eyebrow and one side of his mouth lifted up. "Go ahead. I hate to tell you, but I don't wear anything when I sunbathe. I don't like white streaks."

She knew she wasn't breathing. She just looked at him, stunned.

"You don't have to look at me," he promised wickedly. "And I'll wear a towel out. Will that satisfy your outraged modesty?"

"I've never sunbathed with a naked man...."

"There's a first time for everything." He chuckled at her expression as he turned to go back into his apartment. "Ten minutes."

She wasn't at all sure about this, but they'd grown very close in the time since she'd admitted how she felt about him. They'd talked and shared feelings, about the world and their own lives. He'd told her about his adventures before he'd come to MacFaber, about all the places he'd gone and the things he'd done. She'd listened, fascinated, because he'd lived as she never had. She wondered occasionally how it would be for a man with that kind of background to try to settle down, and it worried her. Wouldn't he be too restless, too used to adventure, to settle for a newspaper and the television in the evenings? Because, inevitably, the newness of marriage would wear off and it would become routine. Unless he loved her, she thought miserably, they might not make it together. Her love for him would hardly be enough in the long run.

She got into the brief black bikini that she'd bought on an impulse at a sale and stared at herself in the mirror. She had a good body, at least, even if she wasn't beautiful, and she blushed, remembering that Jake had seen almost all of it that morning. There was really no reason for her to be shy with him—except that he was going to take all his clothes off, and she felt uncomfortable about that. But he'd talked about a family, and she had to start getting used to him.

She grabbed up the old blanket she used to sunbathe on and carried it outside, taking off her glasses on the way so that she wouldn't have a white streak over her eyes.

She spread out the blanket, grateful all over again for the very secluded backyard that was fenced as well as heavily wooded. No one ever intruded here—probably because the nearest development was a retirement complex for older people, and no children were allowed there.

She lay on her stomach and, minutes later, Jake came out with a beige towel wrapped around his lean hips.

She closed her eyes tightly, hearing his soft laughter as he dropped the towel and stretched out on his stomach beside her.

"Are you planning to have therapy after your wedding night?" he asked dryly.

It disturbed her that he'd said "your" wedding night instead of "our" wedding night. He'd mentioned a baby, so didn't that mean marriage? Perhaps to him it didn't, and that raised even more disturbing questions.

She opened her eyes reluctantly, but all that wasn't blurred was his broad, dark face. "I don't know," she said in a thin voice. "I'm sorry!"

"You'll get used to me. Here. Let me help you out of that."

Before she could speak, his lean fingers were working at laces matter-of-factly, and seconds later, she was as nude as he was, her only coverings trapped under her body. She tensed, but when he stretched back out and sighed, closing his eyes, she let the tension drain out of herself and felt for the first time in her life the unblocked kiss of the sun on her body.

"My goodness," she whispered, feeling languid and oddly sensual.

"Heaven, isn't it?" he murmured. "I used to have so damned many hang-ups about this sort of thing that I couldn't enjoy it. But I spent some time on the Riviera, and you simply can't indulge in modesty on a yacht when everyone else is stripped down."

Her head turned toward him and her eyes opened, wide and curious. "What were you doing on a yacht on the Riviera?" she asked slowly.

There was a pause while he lay there cursing himself silently and wondering how he was going to talk himself out of that stupid slip. There was faint suspicion in her eyes, and he could have kicked himself for what he'd said. Of all the times to let his guard down! What could he say now, without making himself out to be a liar?

Seven

Oh, I get it," Maureen said with a smile. "You worked your way across the south of France as a mechanic!"

"Exactly," he said as smoothly as he could. "Nice guess."

"Have you always been interested in mechanical things?" she persisted, trying not to notice the hard, perfect lines of the masculine body next to hers. Even his legs were tanned like the rest of him, and there was no white streak across his lower spine. He looked broad and fit and extremely sexy.

"I used to take things apart when I was a boy," he murmured.

"I'll bet your parents loved that."

He frowned slightly. "I beg your pardon?"

"Well, taking alarm clocks apart, and lamps and things."

He shifted a little. "I wasn't at home. I was away at school."

Her eyes watched his face. "At a boarding school?" she asked hesitantly.

"It was a school for delinquent boys," he said shortly. "I got in trouble with the law when I was about thirteen and my parents turned me out of the house."

"Oh, Jake," she whispered softly. She reached out a gentle hand and stroked his forearm. She could almost feel the pain radiating out of him at the memory.

"My God, you open me up," he muttered. "I've never told that to another living soul."

"Is it all right if I look smug, then?" she asked with a smile.

He sighed and rolled over onto his side to study her face, enjoying the way she tried not to look at him. She lost the battle, and despite her blurred vision she got an eyeful. She jerked her gaze back up to his face and tried to pretend that her face wasn't scarlet.

"Go ahead. Look at me if you want to," he said gently. "I'm not self-conscious—at least not since I've dropped about fifty pounds," he mused.

"I can't picture you being overweight," she ventured.

"I was fat, honey." He rolled over onto his back and stretched lazily, enjoying the sun on his body. He closed his eyes, giving Maureen the opportunity she was too shy to take while he was watching. He smiled, knowing how fascinating she found him.

And she did. Her eyes lingered helplessly. She'd seen men this way in a magazine that Charlene had brought to work, but never a man in the flesh. Jake was beautifully made. Thick black hair curled down his tanned body to powerful long legs and a blatant masculinity that made her feel weak all over. She'd had a taste of his lovemaking, and she imagined that in bed, he'd be every woman's secret dream. Her body began to throb in the oddest way as she gave her eyes their freedom. He was close enough that most of him didn't blur, and she learned things about him that were faintly shocking when his body began quite suddenly to react to her frank appraisal.

He was studying her, propped up on his forearm so that he could see her face. She looked into his eyes and realized only then that she was propped up, too, and he could see every inch of her.

The strange thing was that she didn't want to lie down again or cover herself. It seemed the most natural thing in the world to be like this with him.

"Come here, little one," he said softly. "Let it happen."

She trembled as his lean hands gently brought her over him. She felt her whole body clench at the feel of warm muscle and abrasive hair tickling her soft skin, but she gave in without a single protest.

He brought her mouth to his and kissed it as he never had before, with tenderness and aching warmth. His hands smoothed over her, drawing her between his hard-muscled thighs, into an embrace that was shocking and sweet and all of heaven.

"Oh, yes," he breathed huskily. His hands went to the base of her spine and held her against him in total intimacy while his hard mouth brushed with maddening leisure at hers.

Her own hands had moved shyly to frame his face and she kissed him back with the same hunger she could feel rippling through his large body.

He eased her onto her back and looked down into her eyes while he touched her, lingering on her small, firm breasts and flat belly. Then his breathing deepened as he began to touch her with infinite care, and she caught his wrist and gasped.

"You're going to belong to me in a very few minutes," he whispered gently. "I have to know how careful I need to be with you. Just relax." She did, shivering as he kissed her and probed gently. "I won't have to hurt you very much," he whispered.

Her eyes opened as his mouth moved down onto her breasts and made her writhe with the sweetest kind of sensual torment. She moaned and bit her lip to stifle the sound.

In the back of her mind there was a last virginal fear of what lay ahead, and a nervousness about being like this with him out in the open. But no one would come, she thought dizzily, and they were totally secluded from the view of any neighbors. . . .

He kissed her lazily as his hips began to move sinuously, his legs tangling with hers, moving against hers in a way that made her body sing with pleasure. She moaned again, because he was using not only his mouth but his whole body—his hands, his legs, his hips—as instruments of pleasure, playing her with consummate skill.

One big hand slid under her head, cradling it, and his eyes looked straight into hers when he moved with a slow purpose that her innocence recognized with faint fear.

"Lie still," he whispered. "I'll be very, very careful."

Her lips pressed together hard and then she gasped softly and winced.

"Just another few seconds, little one," he whispered. His hand tightened under her head. "Don't fight it. . . . Yes!"

She swallowed and breathed quickly, feeling her body absorb him with shock and wonder. Her eyes widened. Her dreams of intimacy hadn't been this staggering. He seemed to know, because his hands and his mouth were slow and tender as he drew her into the soft rhythm with him.

"I'm not...protected," she managed, as the first shock of pleasure began to lift her.

"I know," he breathed. His teeth caught her lower lip and tugged at it gently. His mouth moved against hers, parting her lips. "I want a child," he ground out.

She felt the world going wild with color behind her tightly closed eyelids. Sounds penetrated. Fierce whispers. Rough, rhythmic breathing. The faint cries torn from her throat as the new and staggering pleasure began to build in her and around her. She saw waves of red in her mind, swirling, going faster and faster. Above her, Jake's face was like stone, rigid with building passion. His hands caught hers and locked them to the ground above her head while his muscular body moved with growing fierceness, his weight forcing her deeper into the grass.

She cried out his name suddenly and then she began to sob, because the great surging waves were breaking in her body, crashing, crashing...!

He bit off a word that she barely heard and stiffened even as his breath released and he sank against her with her name torn from him.

She was aware of the weight of him, of the dampness of her body and his, of beads of sweat running down her face. Of exhaustion and such exquisite pleasure, still clinging to her like her damp hair.

His mouth brushed tenderly against her ear, her throat. "We make music together," he murmured. "The sound of two souls joining in ecstasy...."

Her hands touched his face and her eyes opened into his. "I love you," she whispered tiredly.

"I know," he whispered back. The wonder of it was in his eyes, in his smile. He bent and kissed her swollen lips warmly. "Now you have to marry me," he said softly. "You've compromised me. A man has to protect his reputation. I can't have women pointing fingers at me and whispering behind my back that I'm easy."

She laughed with pure delight and hugged him close, burying her face in his damp throat. "I'd marry you right now if I could."

"Monday," he suggested. "We'll have a blood test and get a license...."

"I'll have to ask permission at work to get off."

"No, you won't." He kissed her again, hungrily. His blood began to race all over again. He lifted his head and the teasing vanished. "Let's go and bathe each other. Then I want you in a bed, slowly this time."

She shivered at the mental pictures he was painting. "Again?"

"Yes." He lifted himself away from her and got to his feet, magnificent in his masculinity. He reached down and pulled her up with him. Then, lifting her tenderly, his eyes adoring her, he carried her not into her apartment, but into his, and closed the door.

They slept finally, but it was long after midnight. She woke the next morning with a new soreness in her muscles and vivid memories of the afternoon and night before. She could hardly sit up she was so shaky. Her eyes lit on a bit of paper on the pillow and a black scrawl across it.

"It's all right if you get to work late," Jake had written. "Your boss won't mind. I'll see you after the test flight. Meet me in MacFaber's office. Jake."

She smiled, holding the bit of paper to her lips. Her eye caught something on the back and she turned it over. What was written there made her breath catch.

"If you aren't pregnant this morning, it isn't my fault."

She laughed. So he had meant it. It hadn't been a statement made in passion or to get under her guard. She
stretched and went to look in the mirror, to see if she
looked any different. She didn't, except for some passion
marks in odd places on her creamy body. She flushed and
went to borrow his dressing gown to go back to her own
apartment and dress for work.

She'd always thought that her conscience would beat her
to death if she slept with a man she wasn't married to. But
Jake wanted to marry her. And she loved him, even if he
hadn't been forthcoming about his own feelings. He
couldn't have been so tender with her if he didn't love
her—could he?

They were going to be married in just three days and he
wanted children with her. Everything would be all right.
She'd be Mrs. Jake Edwards.

She hugged that thought to her bosom and rushed inside to dress, casting a rueful glance at the blanket still on
the lawn where they'd made love for the first time. She
went and grabbed up the blanket, his towel and her bikini, and took them inside.

The flight test was already under way when she got to the
plant. They'd brought the Faber jet here to the main administrative offices for its second test flight, and the
grandstand was full of visiting dignitaries. Somewhere in
that gathering, she knew, was the evasive Mr. MacFaber
himself. She wondered if he was holding his breath while
the plane was put through its paces, and she held her own
breath from her vantage point just outside her office.

If anything went wrong this time, the world would end
for some of the employees. She could imagine MacFaber
with a battle-ax, slamming down the halls on both sides
and splitting heads. She didn't see Mr. Blake, her own

boss, and she wondered where he was. Perhaps he was down with the visiting dignitaries.

"How's it going?" Charlene asked breathlessly, standing just beside her.

"So far, so good." Maureen crossed her fingers.

"You look all springlike and breezy today." Charlene grinned, approving the green dress and long, loose hairdo. "You're absolutely radiant."

Maureen smiled. "I'm head over heels in love with one of the mechanics," she confessed. "We're going to get married!"

"One of the mechanics?"

"He's a very nice man and I don't mind living on hamburgers and chips," she assured her friend.

"Is that how I sounded? I didn't mean to." Charlene smiled sweetly. "It's just that one of the mechanics is out on his ear and Mr. Blake's in a lot of trouble. MacFaber was in his office this morning and he called Mr. Blake in. I wasn't eavesdropping, you know, but the office door was open a crack...."

"Well, tell me!"

"Mr. Blake's brother-in-law took it on himself to ignore a design change. He worked in the plant where the Faber jet was assembled." She grimaced. "Mr. Blake finally had to tell MacFaber before something terrible happened. He's been demoted and his brother-in-law has been fired."

"My gosh," Maureen gasped with mingled sorrow for Mr. Blake and relief that Jake wasn't responsible for the problem. "No wonder Mr. Blake looked so worried." That brought to mind her own situation. "Well, who am I working for now?" she asked. "Have I still got a job?"

"Sure. But you won't know who you're working for until MacFaber hires somebody to replace Mr. Blake."

"Have you actually seen MacFaber?" she teased. "I mean, he isn't a figment or anything?"

"Have I seen him!" Charlene looked upward and made a whistling sound. "My gosh, if I weren't an engaged woman...!"

"But you said he was old and ugly." Maureen frowned.

"The last time I saw him, he looked that way. But he's slimmed down and tanned, and at least one of the girls in the typing pool swooned when he walked by. God help the female employees, and I'll bet the lady in South America is crying her eyes out!"

"He sounds fascinating," Maureen said, grinning.

"He is fascinating, except for his temper," the other girl said ruefully. "You can hear him two offices away when he loses it, and he doesn't mind who listens. He's got quite a vocabulary when he gets started."

"It's his corporation," Maureen pointed out. "I guess he was pretty upset about what happened to the Faber jet."

"He wasn't just upset at Mr. Blake's brother-in-law," Charlene murmured. "He was furious at the whole quality-control unit, the design unit, the assembly plant, and assorted other people."

Maureen's eyebrows rose. "Such as?"

"Such as the people who mow the lawn here, the painters who did his office, the carpet layers, two total strangers who happened to walk past his office, and the president."

"My goodness. Were they all responsible for his jet's problems?"

"To hear him tell it, they were. Look!"

She pointed skyward, where the small private-jet prototype was moving like silver grace, sleek and smart and completely in the control of its expert pilot.

"Well, well—" Maureen sighed "—I do believe we have a winner."

"It looks that way," Charlene said, smiling her relief. "Thank God. Maybe this will calm the old man down."

"Is he old?"

"Oh, late thirties, I guess."

"Did you see the detective?" Maureen asked suddenly.

"Yes, indeed, I did." She sighed. "Talk about being overwhelmed with handsome men. He's tall and dark and very, very sexy. I got goose bumps when he spoke to me. Of course, I am an engaged woman," she added seriously.

"But you can still look," Maureen said, smiling.

"That's exactly right. Why do you want to know what the private detective looks like?"

Maureen didn't say. She couldn't very well tell Charlene that she thought she was going to marry him. It wasn't a certain thing yet that Jake was the undercover detective, but she had definite suspicions about it. She smiled to herself as she shook her head at Charlene's question and turned her eyes skyward. It would be exciting, being the wife of a detective. She might even get to help him on a case now and then. The thought brightened her whole day.

Charlene left just after the jet was beginning its descent. Maureen watched the silver bird land and sighed over its grace and beauty. Thank God it had worked this time.

She went back inside, hoping that her job wasn't going to be on the line now that Mr. Blake had been demoted. She had a sudden terrifying thought that Mr. MacFaber might blame her, too. He might think Blake had confided in her and feel that she was in the wrong for not contacting someone about it.

There was little for her to do in her office. Jake had told her to meet him in MacFaber's office, but she hesitated. Everyone would be out at the field with the dignitaries, congratulating each other on the flight. Wouldn't Jake be with MacFaber?

She tidied up, her heart shaking her. After last night, she had a few qualms about being able to look Jake in the eye without blushing. But she was, she reminded herself, twenty-five years old this week, and a capable woman. Then she wondered how she was going to explain her presence in MacFaber's office. Surely if MacFaber came in, she could tell him she was waiting for his detective. He wouldn't eat her, after all.

After freshening her makeup, she ran a brush through her long, loose hair and started out of the office just as the phone rang.

She cursed the interruption, because it was a question about some specs that she had to pull out of the computer. It took a long time and she was flustered and nervous and late when she finished and took the computer offline.

She rushed out the door before anyone else could stop her, down the long hall that led to MacFaber's office. Some of the dignitaries were coming along now, looking pleased and in great spirits. One of the visitors was tall and very good-looking. He glanced at Maureen and inclined his head, but without showing any particular interest.

She glared at his back. He might have noticed that she was sexy and beautiful, she told herself. Jake thought so. Then she thought of Jake as he'd been the day before and blushed with her memories. Even if she died right now, it would be worth it. She felt whole for the first time in her life.

She wondered if Jake felt the same way. He must, because he wanted to marry her and have children with her. Her mind clouded with delightful daydreams. They could live in his apartment and commute to work together. They could go to movies and he could watch her work in the garden patch. On the weekends they could go for long drives and watch movies and play with Bagwell. And when the children came along, Jake would be such a wonderful father. He'd been alone for a long time, and she thought that his parents had probably not wanted him. He was bitter about some of his childhood. She couldn't blame him. At the one time in his life when he'd needed his family, they'd turned their backs on him. She couldn't imagine her own parents doing that. No matter what she'd done, they'd have forgiven her and loved her all the same. She was sorry that Jake wouldn't get to meet them. They'd have liked him. And vice versa.

She knocked on the door of MacFaber's office, to hear Charlene call, "Come in!"

She walked in, looking sheepish at Charlene's raised eyebrows. "I'm supposed to meet him here," she whispered, glancing at the closed door to Charlene's boss's office.

"Him?"

"My fiancé," she reminded the other girl. "He said to meet him in Mr. MacFaber's office after the test flight."

"Oh." Charlene still looked puzzled. "Are you sure?"

Maureen moved closer to the desk, feeling nervous. "Is the detective with him?" she asked hesitantly.

Charlene grinned. "Yes. At least he was when I left. I had to run out for a minute. So that's your big secret. The detective, huh?"

"He was a very good spy," Maureen assured her, her eyes twinkling behind the lenses of her glasses. "And a wonderful person. You can come to the wedding. It's going to be on Monday. And we're going to have a big family and live happily ever after!"

"Sounds like a fairy tale," Charlene said, smiling. "I know just how you feel," she added. "It was that way for me the first few days I was engaged. I never thought it would happen. Just a second."

She touched the intercom button. "Mr. MacFaber? There's a young woman here to see the detective. She said he told her to meet him here."

"Send her in."

The voice was deep and muffled. Maureen took a deep breath and crossed her fingers as she glanced at Charlene.

"He doesn't bite," Charlene promised her. She smiled reassuringly. "You'll like him. Now go in there and get your man. Courage, girl!"

"I don't have much of that, but I'll try. Wish me luck."

"Of course I do."

Maureen reached out for the doorknob and slowly turned it, walking hesitantly into the big, plush office of Joseph MacFaber. It was like entering another world. Everything inside spoke of wealth and position. From the polished oak desk and deep leather chairs to the thick pile carpet and the beige-and-brown color scheme that had a decorator's touch.

On the desk were art objects from around the world and a neat stack of papers. Behind it was a huge leather desk chair, facing the broad windows that overlooked the test field. She couldn't see the man sitting in it.

"I, uh, I'm sorry, but I was told to meet Jake Edwards here, Mr. MacFaber," she said slowly, using the respectful tone she automatically assumed for company officials. "I hope you don't mind. Charlene said that he was in here?" She looked around nervously, but she didn't see the other man. "I think you probably know him by another name. He's your detective . . . I believe?"

It was harder than he'd realized. He stared out the window, hearing her tone change, her nervousness increase. She didn't even sound like the woman he knew. It was as if his position had lifted him out of her reach, made him inaccessible. He grimaced at the difference in her tone, her manner.

"Mr. MacFaber?" she asked again, more nervous than ever, because he wouldn't acknowledge her presence.

"Yes," came a weary, familiar voice from the chair. "I'm MacFaber."

And he whirled the chair around.

Eight

Maureen felt the blood drain from her face. She must be dreaming, she decided. The man in the big chair looked like Jake Edwards, but he was wearing a very expensive blue pinstriped suit and a white silk shirt with a silk floral tie. He looked full of authority and bristling with money.

"I thought it might come as a shock," he acknowledged quietly, and he didn't smile. "But we can deal with it."

"Deal . . . with it?"

He took a cigarette from a metal case and lit it with a gold lighter. "Sit down."

She did, because her legs were threatening rebellion. Her heart shook her with its beat. Her eyes were wide, shocked, wounded.

"You can't be him," she whispered.

"Why not?" He shrugged. "Somebody was trying to sabotage my damned airplane. I thought at first you might know something about it, so I staked you out and pursued you." He took a draw from the cigarette. "But it soon became apparent that you weren't the type to get involved in something that dishonest."

"Then why did you keep seeing me?" she asked. Her world was falling apart and she wanted to scream. She'd given herself to a man who had women like chocolate candies, and her dreams for the future were in ashes. This man wouldn't want a woman like her in a million years. He'd choose a wealthy woman with social position, someone who could function in his world. He wouldn't want a plain nobody of a secretary, even if she had gone crazy and slept with him. And why would he worry about precautions, either, when he could afford a dozen abortions—not that she'd have one.

"You grew on me," he said quietly. "I enjoyed being around you. You gave me lessons in honesty and pride and compassion. I don't think anyone else in my life ever accepted me for what I was instead of what I had, until you did."

"I didn't know who you were," she said with a shaky smile. "You might have told me."

"I wanted to. I couldn't take the risk. You might have let something slip to Blake before I could close in on his in-law."

She lifted her chin. "You didn't trust me."

"Baby, I don't trust anybody, as a rule," he said with a twist of his lips. "Reform school would do that to most thirteen-year-old boys. You came in on my blind side."

She closed her eyes to shut out the pain. "I hope I was worth the time you invested in me, Mr. MacFaber."

"I'm not Mr. MacFaber."

"You aren't Jake Edwards, either!"

"My name is Joseph," he said. "Jake is a nickname the one friend I have in the world uses. Edwards was my mother's maiden name."

She couldn't cry. She didn't dare cry.

He got up from the chair and came around the desk to perch himself on its very edge and watch her, the smoking cigarette in his hand. "As for being worth my time," he said in a voice like cold steel, "that sounds cheap and I don't like it. I never used you, or meant to. I still have every intention of marrying you."

Her lips fell open as she looked up at him. "You can't possibly be serious," she whispered. "My gosh, you're...!"

"I'm a man," he said quietly, his dark eyes holding hers. "I'm alone and I don't like it. You're alone yourself. Why shouldn't we marry?"

"Because you don't love me!"

"Don't I?" he mused. "Can you think of another reason why I'd seduce a virgin?"

She colored and averted her eyes. "That was a mistake," she said huskily. "I know your conscience is probably bothering you, but I don't blame you. And if there's...I mean, if..."

"If you become pregnant?" He let out a cloud of smoke, his broad dark face growing harder by the minute. "What did you have in mind doing?"

She swallowed and closed her eyes. "I don't know. But you don't have to marry me just because I might be pregnant."

"I seem to remember doing my best to make you that way. Several times," he murmured dryly.

She jumped to her feet, only to be caught by the wrist and jerked against him.

"I'll get the license this afternoon and make an appointment with my personal physician for the blood tests in the morning," he said curtly. "Monday, you and I are getting married. Period."

"You can't order me around—!"

He cut her off with his mouth, drowning her in ardor, making her moan with the tempestuous fury of his kiss. "Do you remember what we did at the last?" he whispered into her mouth and captured the tiny cry that accompanied her trembling.

When he let her go, she couldn't stand without his support. She leaned against him, shivering. He wanted her. She knew that. But she didn't think he was really capable of love. He wasn't a vulnerable man, and nothing left a person more helpless than loving someone.

"We shouldn't . . . get married."

"Yes, we should," he said gently. "And every night, I'll love you to sleep. In a few months, you'll give me a child."

She looked up into his dark, quiet eyes curiously. "Do you really want a child so much?"

"I need one," he said.

"Why?"

"Plenty of time for that after we're married." He let her go with a smile. "Go and buy a wedding dress. I'll reimburse you for it, so don't skimp."

"It's so quick," she said vaguely.

"Most good things happen like lightning striking. Are you hungry? We'll go out for lunch, then I've got a full schedule this afternoon. We'll have to see about rings, too."

She was breathless from his commanding attitude. "You were never this busy—"

"I was having a much-needed vacation from business. Now I'm back, and it's not going to slip through my hands again. These damned yes-men aren't going to sink my company," he said with a steely glare.

He didn't even sound like Jake anymore. He sounded cold and ruthless and all business. He made her shiver.

"Let's go." He put out his cigarette and took her arm, half leading, half dragging her to the outer office.

Charlene looked up, her eyebrows arching at the sight of a pale Maureen in MacFaber's grasp.

"We're going out for lunch," he told Charlene. "Get Minnow on the phone and tell him I want him in my office at one sharp. Call Dr. Samson and tell him I'll be in his office at ten tomorrow morning for blood tests for Maureen and myself. Call the courthouse and find out what I have to do to get a marriage license." He stopped to let Charlene catch up. She was flustered and breathless and her eyes kept going helplessly to Maureen. "You can come with us Monday morning. We'll need a witness, so get a girl from the typing pool to fill in for you. Got all that?"

"Yes, Mr. MacFaber," Charlene said smartly, because his eyes had dared her to miss a syllable.

"I'll be back at five before one."

He propelled Maureen out of the office, out of the building, and into a smoke-gray Rolls-Royce waiting with its own uniformed chauffeur.

"Cobb's Grill, Harry," he told the chauffeur and closed the curtain between them and the driver as the car pulled away from the curb. "Now," he said hungrily and turned to Maureen.

By the time they reached the grill, her lipstick was gone and her body was racked with shudders of aching need despite the fulfillment he'd given her the night before. She clung to him, but he put her gently away with a rueful smile, looking totally unruffled.

"Fix your makeup, baby," he murmured, smiling at her abandoned look. "We wouldn't want to shock the other diners, would we?"

"You're . . . just incredible," she said unsteadily as she tried to repair the damage he'd done in the lighted make-up mirror. "You aren't even ashamed of tricking me, deceiving me. . . ."

"You don't give a damn about all that," he murmured, watching her lazily. "You love me too much to care what I've done. And you'll marry me for the same reason."

"Pure conceit," she began.

He touched her mouth with his forefinger. "Do you think so? Suppose I pull you down in this seat and have Harry go for a long walk?" he taunted.

"You wouldn't dare! Not in front of a restaurant!"

"We have curtains," he remarked, indicating them. His dark eyes narrowed playfully. "Of course, you'd have to bite your tongue and hold back those exciting little noises you make when I take you."

Her face flamed. "Jake!"

He laughed. "No, I wouldn't do that to you. Not here. But you do rise so beautifully to the bait, little one." He leaned forward and kissed her nose. "Now stop worrying. We've already got more going for us than most engaged couples. Let's have champagne and toast our future."

"Are we really going to have one?" she asked sadly. "I'm all wrong for a man like you."

"Bull. Come on."

Harry opened the door and Jake helped her out onto the sidewalk. When he escorted her into the restaurant, she felt every eye on her. Probably half these people knew Mac-Faber and were wondering what in the world he was doing with this plain, ordinary woman. Most of the women were wearing designer dresses and suits, and dripping diamonds. She didn't need to be told that in a restaurant like this, you didn't ask for prices before you ordered.

They were seated at a good table, where MacFaber proceeded to order for her with a nonchalance that dared her to protest. She felt as if he'd already taken her over, lock, stock and barrel, and she was going to be little more than a possession for the rest of her life.

When she'd dreamed of marrying him, this hadn't been part of the dream. She'd built her dreams around a man who worked at an ordinary job, liked the same things she did, and wanted a normal life. But she wouldn't be marrying Jake Edwards. She was marrying a rich corporate executive who was used to slinging out orders and cutting off professional heads. How in the world was she going to survive it?

"Stop brooding," he taunted as she picked at her food. "I haven't grown fangs in the past hour."

"Is that how I look?" she asked, her voice subdued. "I'm sorry. It's just such a shock. I was sure at first that you were the saboteur, and then I was sure you were the detective trying to catch him. I never dreamed that you were Mr. MacFaber himself."

He took a sip of the excellent wine he'd been served with his fish and stared at her across the top of it. "My family was wealthy," he said. "But money never made me happy. I had parents who hated each other—and me—and a childhood I wouldn't wish on my worst enemy. If it hadn't been for a particularly understanding policeman who took me under his wing, my life would have been in such a tangle that money wouldn't have helped me."

Her shoulders shifted and she sipped her coffee. "It's just that I had a totally different picture of you," she said. "And of what being married to you would be like." She smiled shakily. "I don't mix very well with people. I don't know the right utensils to use at fancy dinners. I look like what I am—an ordinary woman with a middle-class background. Your friends would look at us and wonder if you'd lost your mind. I won't fit into your world."

That was the same thing he'd said to himself at the beginning, and he still had some lingering doubts. But he enjoyed Maureen. She fulfilled him as no other woman ever had, she was good company, and she was healthy enough to give him an heir. He leaned back in his chair and studied her downcast face.

"I have only one real friend," he remarked. "His name is John Abernathy and he lives in Phoenix. He'll like you." His sensuous mouth curled into a smile. "As for the rest, you'll learn as you go along. I'm filthy rich, you know. People tend to overlook things when they're currying favor."

"You sound very cynical," she said.

"I am cynical," he affirmed. He tossed down the rest of his wine and put the glass gently on the table. "Life has made me that way. You're the only human being I know, besides John, who looked at me and didn't see a dollar sign."

"I didn't know you were rich, though," she said. "Maybe it would have been different if I'd met you as you are now."

His eyebrows arched. "Trying to run me off?" he asked, seeing right through her fear. "It won't work. What you gave me last night turned me inside out. I can't live without it, and you're obviously not cut out to live with me in sin."

She colored. "I could move back to Louisiana...."

"Go ahead. I've got a corporate office there. I'll switch headquarters." He smiled at her irritation. "I like fresh seafood."

"You aren't being reasonable," she began.

"It doesn't get me anywhere," he said. "The steam-roller approach always works best in the long run. Have some dessert," he added as the waiter approached with the dessert trolley.

She chose an éclair and ate it while he munched on a cherry tart. "You see?" She sighed. "We don't even like the same desserts. Marrying you would be a disaster. We'd be divorced—"

"No, we won't. I don't believe in divorce, so if you marry me, you're stuck with me."

"I'll look silly trying to drive a Rolls-Royce."

"Honey, you don't drive the Rolls. Harry drives the Rolls. That's why I hired him." He finished his tart. "I wrapped two of them around a telephone pole and my board of directors surrounded me and threatened to quit en masse if I did it again. So I hired a chauffeur."

"They must care about you," she ventured.

"They care about the way I run the corporation," he corrected. "I've shown a profit every year, and I've made some successful innovations on existing designs."

"Why not make new ones?" she asked curiously, because she had very little insight into designing. The corporation was so big that no one employee knew a lot about anything except his own area of expertise.

"Listen. If you design a new airplane, the law leaves you wide open to lawsuits if anything goes wrong with it. It's not so risky to alter an existing design."

"Oh. I see."

"It's not my fault the whole country's gone lawsuit crazy," he said. "Some of them are justified, but a lot of the time, it's just some lazy so-and-so trying to live off someone else.''

"Do you make design changes yourself?" she asked, curious.

He chuckled. "I'm not going to take the credit for that. I have an excellent design staff and some brilliant electronics people. We have bull sessions. The end result comes from all of us, not any one person."

She could see how his company had grown and why. He was a team player, not an autocrat.

"Why have you stayed away from the corporation so much?"

He sighed. "Did they tell you that my mother was killed in an automobile accident last year, and that I was driving?"

"I heard it," she said. "I'm very sorry."

"Up until then, I was sure that I hated both my parents. My mother was a snob. She had no time for ordinary people, and she hated anything less than the best. She wasn't that crazy about me, either. We went to a party together, and she drank a little more than she was used to." His eyes darkened and narrowed. "We argued about the flight home the next day. She grabbed the steering wheel. It was dark and we were going around a hairpin curve." His big shoulders lifted and fell. "I woke up in a French hospital, with three ribs broken and some minor internal injuries. When they told me she was dead, I think I went a little mad. I spent the next year in the most reckless ways I could think of. I couldn't help feeling responsible."

She slid her hand hesitantly over his big one, tingling at the contact. "You couldn't know she was going to grab the wheel." His hand curled around her fingers, warm and strong. His dark eyes searched her soft ones. "Maybe not." He laughed bitterly. "I used to lie awake at night when I was a boy, trying to figure out what I'd done to make my parents hate me so. They never paid me much attention unless I did something terrible or embarrassed them. I wouldn't conform to the image they had of their only child, you see. I always wondered what it would feel like to be loved and wanted."

"Our children will know," she said, her voice quiet and serious. "And so will you."

He had to clamp down hard on his emotions to keep them in check. He hadn't counted on having someone around who loved him openly and wasn't ashamed to admit to that kind of weakness. He still couldn't. Not verbally. He'd been taught by experts that vulnerabilities were easily attacked.

"How many children are we going to have?" he asked dryly, sidestepping the emotional moment.

She smiled shyly. "How many do you want?"

His fingers caressed hers, savoring their silky softness, their elegant length. "Two or three, I guess. Assorted." He frowned. "We need to go look at rings."

She caught her breath. "Rings?"

"An engagement ring and two wedding bands.... Are you finished?"

No sooner had she nodded than he held up a hand and the waiter instantly produced the check. It was taken care of and they were in the Rolls—Harry seemed to always be waiting patiently—and on their way to the finest jeweler's in town.

Maureen had her eye on a very small diamond in a Tiffany setting with a simple matching gold band. She could see by Jake's scowl that she wasn't going to get it.

With a long-suffering sigh, he positioned her in front of the case holding the most expensive wedding sets in the store.

"No arguments," he said. "I'm worth millions. I can afford a good stone, and you're going to have one," he added doggedly, "if I have to sit on you while Mr. Tyler fits you with it."

Mr. Tyler, an older, long-married man, beamed with approval. Mr. MacFaber was one of his best customers, although this was certainly the first time the aircraft tycoon had bought anything for a young lady. Not at all a ladies' man was Mr. MacFaber, he thought approvingly.

Maureen still hesitated, but he wore her down. She wound up with a two-karat diamond in a Tiffany setting and a matching wide gold band studded with diamonds. The whole thing cost thousands of dollars, and Jake didn't bat an eyelash as he handed his gold credit card to the delighted jeweler.

Jake's own band was a simple plain gold one.

"I didn't know if you'd want to wear one," she said hesitantly.

He glanced down at her while Mr. Tyler polished and boxed the wedding set. "Why wouldn't I?" he asked with a faint smile. "It's my first marriage, too."

She shrugged, hesitating over something she'd wanted to ask him from the minute she'd known who he really was. "It was just a thought." She looked up and sighed. "Jake, what about the lady in South America?" she blurted out, reddening.

Mr. Tyler came back before he could say anything, offering congratulations along with the sales slip and the merchandise. Jake thanked him, escorted Maureen out and put her in the back seat of the Rolls.

"Back to the office, Mr. MacFaber?" Harry asked, once they were inside.

"No." MacFaber loosened his tie with a heavy breath. "We've got a half hour before I have to be back. Drive around somewhere."

"Outside town?" Harry asked hopefully, his dark eyes twinkling under his cap. He was an older man, not over-the-hill, but mature and lean and very capable at the wheel.

"Outside town will do fine, Harry," MacFaber said. He closed the curtain with a grin. "He hates traffic," he told Maureen. He lowered his voice. "Back in the fifties, he was a wheelman for a robbery ring."

Her face brightened. "Was he, really?"

He chuckled. "Any of the people I associate with would be horrified."

"Oh, I like scalawags," she said. "I've led such a sheltered life that I've never really known any except Mr. Dunagan back in Louisiana. He spent two years in jail for forgery. But he was small-time compared to Harry, I guess."

He leaned back against the leather upholstery, feeling relaxed and very satisfied. He opened the jewelry box and brought out the solitaire. "Give me your hand."

She slid it into his and watched him put the ring on her engagement finger. It looked elegant and beautiful and out of place there, but he didn't seem to think so. He brought her hand to his lips and kissed it gently.

"You're mine, now," he said, meeting her eyes levelly. "Since yesterday afternoon on that blanket, you belong to me, and I won't ever let you go."

"I'm glad," she said breathlessly. "I'll try to be the kind of wife you want...."

"You just be yourself, baby," he said, smiling. "That'll do."

He smelled of expensive cologne and she wanted to curl up in his lap and close her eyes and doze, but that would be impractical. Girls didn't just crawl into the laps of aircraft magnates and sleep. Not in the back seats of Rolls-Royces during business hours, anyway.

"What are you thinking?" he asked.

"That I'd like to lie in your arms and sleep," she said, and laughed self-consciously. "It's been a long morning."

"And a short night," he mused, smiling tenderly at her hot cheeks. He held out his arms. "Come here. I can't think of anything I'd rather do."

She slid across his lap and pillowed her cheek on his jacket, inhaling the delicious masculine scent of him with her eyes closed while his big hand touched her hair.

"Jake?"

"Hmm?" he murmured.

"What about the lady in South America?"

He laughed softly. "You won't quit, will you?" He tilted her face up to his. "Do you remember what I told you? About how many years it had been since I'd been intimate with a woman?" he asked gently. "I wasn't kidding. If you want the truth, until you came along I had every fear that I was getting impotent. No one could arouse me—not even the lady from South America, although she tried hard enough."

Her face brightened. "Really?"

He laughed and bent to brush his mouth gently over hers. "Really. And now, I don't want anyone but you," he breathed. "Because what you do with me in bed is almost sacred. You make me want a family and a house—My God, I don't have one!" he exclaimed and sat up, almost unseating her.

"A house?" she echoed.

"A house! I sold the one I had when I went to Europe. The duplex is the only place we have to live." He moved her off his lap. "No, that won't do. We can't live in the duplex. Kids need a lot of space to play in."

"Jake, you won't buy anything terribly expensive?" she asked apprehensively.

"No, of course not," he said nonchalantly. "I don't like pretentious places any more than you do."

"We can stay in the duplex for the time being." He was thinking aloud. "We'll go house hunting tomorrow."

"Do you mind Bagwell?" she asked.

"Of course not. We'll have an aviary built for him, too, so he can spend the summer months outside. He'll like that."

She sighed with relief. "Whose apartment are we going to stay in until we're married?"

He looked down at her solemnly. "You in yours, me in mine." He touched his finger to her tremulous mouth. "I still feel bad about the way things happened, although I don't regret what we gave each other for a second. I think we need to behave ourselves until the vows are spoken."

"You're very conventional in some ways," she murmured, secretly relieved, because her conscience had been working overtime despite his proposal and the immediate marriage.

"I always was. In some ways," he agreed. He checked his watch. "As much as I hate to, I have to get back. I'll be tied up all day and most of the night. Wait up for me, so that I can kiss you good-night when I get home."

"I'll have a meal waiting, if you like."

He shook his head. "I'll have supper out." He frowned. "Cooking is something you won't do much of after we're married. I like having a French chef in the kitchen. We'll have maids, too, and a housekeeper. You'll have time to enjoy yourself and do what you like. No more working. You can put in your notice today."

She started to speak, but he was already giving Harry instructions. She sat back, worrying. He was mapping out a very unsatisfactory future for her. She loved him, and she wanted very much to live with him and be his wife. But he was going to rob her of the things she'd always expected to go with that wonderful dream of being a wife and mother.

He was going to surround her with servants, take away her job and make her into a homebody. That wasn't bad, of course, and she'd enjoy some leisure time. But what was she going to do with her days? He seemed to be always on the move, and business might keep him away for days or weeks at a time. It was going to be a hard enough life with those absences, without having too much free time to brood over missing him.

She didn't say another word about it, but she went back to her office in a brown study, with her heart around her ankles. Life had been so much simpler when she was engaged to a mechanic who came home on time every day and liked to go bowling in an old rusted-out pickup truck.

Nine

Charlene sneaked out of MacFaber's office and into Maureen's while he was occupied with his one o'clock appointment, on the pretext of getting herself a cup of coffee.

She closed the door quickly behind her and just stood there, shaking her head. "The detective, you said?" she reminded her friend, with great, curious eyes.

Maureen had had her head in her hands and she barely looked up. "You aren't any more surprised than I am. First I thought he was an industrial spy. Then I thought he was a mechanic. Then I thought he was the private detective. In the meantime, he was eating breakfast with me and playing with my parrot and taking me to the movies." She stared blankly at Charlene. "He didn't *look* like a millionaire."

"No wonder you were so white in the face," Charlene said, grinning. "My gosh, MacFaber himself! You're the

ninth wonder of the world this afternoon, and I'm a ce-
lebrity because I'm your friend." She laughed. "One of
the girls in the typing pool wants to know if she can have
your autograph. She said to tell you that she believes in
fairy tales, now."

Maureen smiled in spite of herself. "It might seem like
one, but it's a lot more difficult to live up to Prince
Charming than you might think. He took me to lunch at
one of those expensive restaurants and people looked at
him like they thought he was crazy." She frowned
thoughtfully. "Now, there's a possibility...."

"MacFaber isn't crazy. He makes other people crazy,"
Charlene assured her. "Can I see your ring?"

Maureen held out her hand. The diamond caught the
light and exploded into color like a prism of ice.

"It's incredible," Charlene exclaimed with a sigh.

"My life is incredible." Maureen shook her head. "I
can't imagine how I'm going to cope. I love him, you
know, but it's going to be pure culture shock."

"All you have to do is smile and spend money," Charlene assured her.

But after the other woman had gone, Maureen's smile
fell into a frown. Money wasn't that important in her life.
Love was. She wanted Jake to herself. She didn't want to
have to share him with business, so that she came out on
the short end of the stick as far as time shares went. She
wanted to go places with him and have time to just sit and
talk. She wanted to relax with him in the evenings. All that
would have satisfied her a lot more than the latest designer dresses and plenty of spending money. She had a
feeling that millionaires' wives were the loneliest people on
earth.

She typed out her resignation and, since she had no one
to give it to, she laid it on Mr. Blake's old desk before she

went home. She patted her little VW as she got into it and had a sudden cold thought that it would be one of the casualties of her new life-style, because Jake Edwards might not have minded it in his driveway, but she was sure Joseph MacFaber wasn't going to want it in his garage next to the Rolls.

"Don't you worry," she told it when she parked it in the driveway, patting its faded dash. "I'll hide you out in the woods if I have to, but they're not going to consign you to the garbage dump."

She went into the apartment and fed Bagwell, who enthused over the carrot she'd cut up for him and made soft purring sounds to himself as he ate it.

She ruffled his green head and cooked herself a bowl of chili. It would have been nice if she'd had someone to eat it with.

As she savored her spicy meal, she wished her parents were still alive. It would have been nice to call and tell them about her engagement, about Jake. They'd have asked about him, and she'd have told them that he was very handsome and very strong and that he had a kind heart. Then they'd have asked if he could support her, and she'd have smiled as she told them what he did for a living.

The thought made her sad. Tears ran down her cheeks and fell onto the place mat. It seemed ironic that a person could wait years for something incredible to happen, and then when it did, there was nobody to tell.

She washed her bowl and poured herself another cup of coffee. The one bright spot in her life was that Jake was going to marry her. She looked at the engagement ring glittering on her finger and smiled, pressing her lips to it. He wanted to spend his life with her and give her children. She flushed, remembering what he'd said the day before, his body so tender as it overwhelmed hers, his hands gentle, preparing her for the shock of possession. It had been easier than she'd ever dreamed and more powerful and awesome than anything she'd ever felt. She was his now, and he was hers. Even if she only saw him once in a while, it was enough that she could live with him. And he did want her, if nothing else. Maybe someday he'd even learn to love her.

It was almost midnight when he knocked on her kitchen door. She was still wearing her jeans and T-shirt, curled up on the couch watching the late show since the next morning was Saturday. Bagwell's cage was covered and he was asleep.

"You look terrible," she told the weary man outside the door.

"I feel terrible," he said, even his voice drooping. "I've just now got out of another meeting. You can't imagine how complicated it is to have a production error that isn't found in the early stages of testing."

She stood back to let him enter the apartment. His tie was hanging loosely around his neck and his jacket was looped over his shoulder by a finger. His shirt was open at the throat. His dark eyes were bloodshot and there were new lines in his broad, deeply tanned face.

"Do you want coffee, or would you rather lay your head in my lap and go to sleep?" she asked gently.

He pulled her against him and kissed her with lazy tenderness. "Can I have both?"

"With my blessing."

She poured him a cup of black coffee and watched him slump beside her on the sofa. His thick dark hair was tousled. He had a shadow of beard on his square jaw. He looked as if he'd been run over by a big truck, and she said so.

He laughed. "I guess I do. I feel that way. Damned red tape." He sipped his coffee with his eyes barely open. "The blood test is at ten in the morning. We can't forget."

"We won't." She smoothed back his unruly hair, loving the freedom to touch him. "Poor, tired man."

He caught her hand and pressed it to lips that were hot from the coffee. "I've never had anyone to come home to before." His head turned and his dark eyes searched her face. "It feels nice, Maureen."

"I'm glad. I've never had anyone come home to me before, and that feels nice, too," she said, smiling at him. "I thought I'd live and die alone." Her eyes lowered to the neck of his shirt, and she was amazed at how easy it was to talk to him. She wasn't even embarrassed about the intimacy they'd shared. It seemed natural and right, a part of their togetherness. "I can get contact lenses, if you'd like," she ventured. "They might improve me a little."

"You don't need improving," he replied, smiling back at her. "I like you as you are, glasses and all."

That lifted her spirits. "How about if I have my hair permed and tinted green and pink, then?" she added with a grin. "I could throw wild parties with punk-rock themes and make your name a household word."

He laughed. It surprised him that he should do it so easily with her, when he'd hardly laughed in his life before she came along. "I don't care what you do," he replied. "But I'm not tinting my hair pink and green for you."

"It would bring you closer to your employees."

"Certainly—they'd be after me with a fishnet!"

She laid her head against his big arm with a sigh. "I'm a different person when I'm with you," she remarked quietly. "You bring out qualities I didn't know I had. I'm really very shy around people as a rule."

"You were shy last night, kitten," he whispered at her temple. "Most of the time, anyway."

She flushed and buried her face against him. "Stop."

She looked up into his eyes with those memories in hers, too. "How could you be that tender after two whole years of going without a woman?" she asked huskily.

"You were a virgin," he said simply. His mouth brushed hers softly. "I couldn't very well put my own pleasure above yours, could I?"

"From what I've read, some men do."

"I care about you," he whispered. He teased her mouth with his. "Was it what you expected?"

"Not really," she confessed shyly. "I could never have imagined doing that outside in broad daylight."

"We were safe enough. No one ever visits either one of us, and there aren't any curious neighbors or children around. We're very secluded here." He searched her eyes and his own began to darken. "I enjoyed you more than you'll ever know. But I want you to know that I didn't plan what happened between us. I never meant it to go that far, but once I felt your body against mine with nothing in the way, it was just impossible for me to stop."

She smiled to herself. "Every time I remember what we did last night, I want you again," she whispered.

His hand caught her hair and held her head where he wanted it as he bent and covered her mouth with his. He brought her closer, building the kiss until she was as hungry as he was, until his tongue penetrated her mouth and she moaned, wanting his hands on her.

"I want you, too," he whispered into her mouth. "But this is all we're going to do. If you want me again, you're going to have to marry me first."

"Blackmail," she moaned.

"Call it what you will." His mouth bit into hers roughly and then he sat up and finished his coffee. "I can't remember when I was this tired. I've got to have some sleep." He looked down at her with a rueful smile. "I don't want to go home, but if I stay here, we'll have each other before morning. I can't sit within a foot of you without catching fire."

"That's very flattering."

"It's very incapacitating, too," he said, grinning.

She laughed as he stood up and stretched lazily. "You can sleep until nine, and I'll phone you. We'll get our blood tests and apply for the license—"

"It's Saturday," she pointed out.

"I'm a millionaire," he reminded her. "Money opens doors."

"I guess it does," she said vaguely.

"Besides all that, Saturday isn't a national holiday."

She made a face at him. "Don't expect me to think. I've had a shocking day."

"And a shocking night before it?" he mused.

She glared. "You weren't always experienced," she accused.

"No, I wasn't. My first time, I chickened out and ran," he confessed with a chuckle. "I don't know who was more shocked—the woman or me."

"Obviously there was a next time," she murmured, lowering her eyes. "You know too much for a man who's never indulged."

"I'm a man," he said, pulling her up to stand in front of him. "I had to learn how to be one. But I never got a woman pregnant or seduced virgins." He smiled ruefully. "Until yesterday, anyway."

"I'm sorry. I don't mean to sound jealous."

"I like having you jealous," he said quietly. "And if you want the truth, there haven't been that many women. I've been very selective, and I haven't wanted a close relationship. Not until you came along and knocked me off my feet."

"I'm not pretty...."

"Honey, you're a knockout," he said, his voice deep and velvety. "It's what's inside that makes you beautiful. You've got a heart the size of Kansas, and when you love, you do it with your soul. I wouldn't trade you for Helen of Troy."

"Oh, Jake," she whispered.

He kissed her roughly and pushed her away. "Stop looking at me like that," he ground out. "I'm already shaking, I want you so badly."

"We could—"

"No, we couldn't," he said shortly. "I'll let myself out. Go to bed. We've got a big day ahead of us."

He turned toward the door, but he hesitated at it, regretting his sharp tone. "Men get grumpy when they're frustrated," he said uncomfortably. "I didn't mean to snap at you."

"I know," she said and smiled gently. "Good night."

He caught his breath at the radiance in her face. His dark eyes slid over her body in the simple T-shirt and jeans, and he almost groaned aloud remembering how it looked and felt and tasted without clothing. He remembered her eyes looking up at him, wide with wonder and pleasure, the sounds breaking from her tight throat, the feel of her soft hands on the strained muscles of his back....

"Good night," he choked and got out quickly.

They had the blood tests the next morning and got the license. The ceremony was arranged for Monday. It would have to be a civil service, Jake informed her, because he had to fly to Chicago that night for a meeting.

Maureen was shocked that he couldn't even find one full day off to get married. "But it will be our wedding day," she said hesitantly.

He stared at her with narrowed eyes. "I'm not a 'mechanic' anymore. I head a giant corporation, and I've already had hell keeping it together because I spent the last year delegating too much authority. I've spent the past few weeks finding out why my jet wouldn't fly. I'm out of time, Maureen. The honeymoon will have to wait."

"Then, can I come to Chicago with you?" she asked hopefully. "I'll be very quiet...."

He moved closer to her and took her gently by the arms. "I don't like it any more than you do. You can come if you like, but I'll be gone almost all night. We'll see very little of each other. And I have to be there four days or so—what about Bagwell?"

She grimaced. "I can't board him. He'd die away from me. And I can't take him with me...."

"We've got our whole lives ahead of us, baby," he said quietly. "These few days aren't going to matter. Especially," he added ruefully, "when we've already jumped the gun and had our wedding night."

She colored and lowered her eyes to his chest. "Yes, I know. I ... still feel rather guilty about that."

"You might not believe it, but so do I," he said surprisingly. "That's why I've insisted that we wait until we're married. Don't make such a big thing of it, okay? It's just for a few days. I'll call you when I can. Be a good girl and use the time to wind things down at the office and get your gear together. When I come home we'll go find a house to live in."

She gave in, because what else was there to do? She'd known when she agreed to marry him that his main interest was his corporation. She could hardly ask him to throw it to the wolves just for her.

"Okay," she agreed and tried to smile. "I won't make a fuss."

"I didn't think you would," he said easily. "You aren't the demanding type. That's one reason I married you. I don't want a woman who clings and can't manage if I'm not home every night. That's why I've never married before. I like my freedom."

She remembered those words with a shudder when she went to bed. He liked his freedom and the corporation came first. Where was she going to fit into his life? Was she going to fit at all?

He was giving her an impossible choice. She wanted to marry him, because she loved him. But it wasn't working out the way she'd expected.

She went to church alone on Sunday. He hadn't called, and he didn't answer his phone when she tried to call him. But he phoned her after church and agreed rather reluctantly to come to supper that night, but he was preoccupied and left early to make a long-distance phone call. Even his good-night kiss was absent, as if he'd only just remembered that he needed to kiss his fiancée good-night.

Maureen was getting more nervous by the minute. She didn't sleep that night, worrying about whether or not to go through with the wedding. MacFaber didn't love her, and that was one strike against them already. They had different backgrounds and different life-styles, and that was another. She didn't know if they had any chance at all, but she loved him too much to back down and call it off. Maybe things would change, she thought. Maybe he'd fall in love with her and want her so badly that he couldn't bear to spend a night away from her. She hugged that thought to herself as she finally fell asleep, long after midnight.

They were married at ten o'clock in the morning by a justice of the peace, with Charlene and one of the executive vice presidents—Charlene's fiancé—as witnesses. Maureen cried at the simple beauty of the service, standing proudly beside Jake in a white suit and white hat with a tiny veil. When he put her wedding ring on her finger and kissed her, the tears were still there, but she smiled through them with pure joy.

There wasn't time for a reception, so they thanked the witnesses and went home so that Jake could pack for the flight to Chicago.

She'd half expected that once they were in her apartment he might want her, since they were married now. But he sat down at her table while she made coffee, and his eyes stared blankly into space as if he were thinking.

"Well, we're married," she said when she'd put coffee and rolls in front of him and was sitting across from him.

"So we are." He sipped his coffee. "Do you want to go house hunting while I'm away, or do it when I come home?"

"I'd like to go with you," she said. "It wouldn't be fair for me to pick out someplace alone."

"Why not?" he asked with raised eyebrows. "After all, you're the one who'll be there most of the time. I'll be away sometimes for a week or two at a stretch, and most nights I work until nearly midnight. On weekends I have business meetings and conferences, and even when I'm home, I'll have reports and statements to go over and decisions to make."

She could have cried. It was her wedding day, and he was already talking about leaving her alone most of the time in the future. "Do we get any time together, Jake?" she asked miserably.

He didn't like the hurt look in her eyes or the plaintive tone. He hadn't thought of Maureen as a clinging woman, and he didn't think he could manage to live with her if she turned into one. Better, he thought, to nip this in the bud now. He glared at her. "I don't make the rules. A corporation runs on the brains of its management, and I've spent too much time delegating responsibility. I did it so well that it almost lost the business for me. I can't fall back into that rut again. I've tried to explain to you that my corporation is the biggest part of my life. I hope you don't expect to replace it with a few pleasant hours in your bed?"

She went red. "I don't understand."

"What I mean, Mrs. MacFaber," he said with a mocking smile, "is that you have a sweet body and I enjoy it very much. But sex is only one small part of my life, not the whole ball game."

Her world was coming down around her ears. She was hearing him tell her quite plainly that he'd only married her because he enjoyed her body in bed; that outside it, he had no interest in her.

"Is that why you married me?" she faltered. "Because you wanted to sleep with me?"

He took a harsh breath. That wasn't how he'd meant to put it. She was backing him into a corner. "You know why I married you," he said, his tone curt and commanding. "I enjoy being with you—when you aren't giving me the third degree." He stood up. "I'd better get packed. Listen," he added, pausing at the door to look back at her with cold, chilling eyes, "don't start trying to tie me down. I've done things my own way for a long time. The last thing I need is a possessive woman. Do we understand each other?"

She had to grit her teeth to keep from making a scene. It was her wedding day, and he was treating her like an unwanted piece of furniture.

"Yes, I understand," she said, lowering her eyes to the floor. "You don't even...even want me?" she whispered.

The answer seemed to take forever. "Now, you mean?" he asked.

She nodded, her cheeks reddening.

He laughed mirthlessly. "It won't work," he said coolly. "You won't convince me to take you to Chicago that way," he went on when he saw her perplexed stare.

"I never thought of that," she responded miserably. "It's our wedding day. I thought you... Never mind."

"No, I'm not eaten up with desire," he said. He checked his watch. "Even if I were, I don't have time for it. I'll see you Thursday."

She started to speak to ask if he wasn't going to kiss her goodbye, but in his present mood, it wouldn't do any good to ask. He'd just bite her head off.

She watched him go out the door with a sinking heart. She was Mrs. Joseph MacFaber. She knew absolutely nothing about his parents, except that they'd let him go to reform school. She didn't even know their names. She didn't know where Jake was born, where he grew up, or what kind of toothpaste he used. She knew almost nothing about him. And right now she was wondering what had possessed her to let him rush her into marriage.

It was possible that he was old-fashioned enough to feel guilty that he'd seduced her. He said he wanted her, but he certainly hadn't acted like it today. His mind had been totally on work; not on her. He was leaving to spend the week in Chicago alone, leaving her here by herself only hours after they'd been married.

She glared at the closed door. He was being unreasonable. She ought to go over to his apartment and tell him so. But he was probably too busy packing to listen.

Well, if he expected her to sit here for four days while he went to Chicago on business, he was in for a surprise. She wasn't going to be his doormat. If he wanted a society wife, he was going to have one. She'd have herself done over and buy some clothes, then she'd start looking for houses. She'd engage her own staff, thank you very much, and if he didn't like it, he could divorce her and go and live with his company!

She felt much better with her mind made up. The only thing was they didn't have a joint bank account and she had only the money in her savings account. She pulled out her bankbook and grimaced at the small figure in it.

So much for having herself made over. Maybe she could set her hair or something and paint her body green and make a toga out of one of the colored bedsheets and meet him like that at the airport. The reporters would probably love that. She'd make all the evening editions.

She laughed at her own absurd idea. No, she couldn't do that even to MacFaber. It would have to be something less spectacular.

For one thing, she decided, she could tear up her resignation and keep her job. The way things were going, she might need it until she could find a job working for somebody else. If MacFaber was going to relegate her to the outfield of his life, she'd need something to occupy her time. He wasn't going to let her run the house or cook for him, and he'd just said that he'd only want her now and again in bed, so she might as well work.

"Car-rot!" Bagwell called from the kitchen table.

"You'll turn orange," she cautioned as she handed him another carrot and began to prepare a beef stew. "I'll get to eat this myself, you realize," she told the big green bird. "Bagwell, do you like beef stew?"

Too busy with the carrot in his claw, he didn't answer her.

She started the stew and sat down to watch television. There was a movie on and she stared at it blankly, thinking that, of all the wedding days in the history of the world, this must surely be the very worst.

Maybe Jake would come back by the apartment and apologize. Maybe he'd kiss her goodbye hungrily and decide he couldn't bear Chicago without her, even for a few days. Maybe he'd rush in on his knees with passionate declarations of love.

Bagwell stared at her, because she was laughing a little hysterically.

She got herself back under control, but as the minutes ticked by, there was still no sign of her new husband. Finally, unable to stand the waiting any longer, she picked up the telephone and dialed his number. It rang and rang and rang.

She hung up and went outside, around to his apartment. It was locked, and the lights were all out. He'd gone without a single word, as if she no longer existed for him.

Probably, she thought miserably, she didn't. Marrying him had been her biggest mistake. But she didn't have to compound it by mooning over him. She'd make the best of her situation until she could decide where to go, because she certainly didn't want to live with a man who could treat her like that.

She'd go to work tomorrow, she decided. Then she'd give herself a few days to decide what she was going to do with her life. One thing was certain: she wouldn't take a red cent from MacFaber, so he wouldn't have to worry about alimony or anything.

The only other worry would be pregnancy. She hadn't taken precautions and neither had he. A child was a definite possibility, and she remembered that he'd said he wanted one. Then why had he treated her like this, on their wedding day? Had he been temporarily insane when he proposed? Try as she might, she couldn't come up with a better explanation for his behavior.

He'd lived alone for a long time, she recalled, and that was by choice. What if he couldn't adjust to another person? And he might have some real doubts about her ability to handle his house and servants and give parties and do all the other things expected of a society wife.

She pursed her lips. She could go to the library, she supposed, and read some books on parties and such. She could check out some biographies of well-known hostesses. Now there was a thought. She'd do it, she decided, the very next day. Before she cut and ran, she would show MacFaber that she wasn't too stupid to organize a dinner party or motivate staff or be a successful hostess. And she would.

Ten

Jake's trip to Chicago lasted one day longer than he'd expected. It was Saturday morning, five days after the wedding, and Maureen was waiting for Harry to pick her up in the Rolls, as Jake had arranged by phone, and take her to the airport to meet Jake's plane. He'd promised to phone her, and he had. Once. It had been a quick, terse conversation, with neither of them giving an inch. Maureen had hardly slept all night after it.

She'd taken back her resignation and kept on with her job. If she and Jake were going to have a fight, she reasoned, it might as well be a proper one. She wasn't going to become a glorified mistress. If he wanted a wife, he was going to have to let her be one, in every sense of the word—a cook, housekeeper and lover. She wouldn't settle for being made a convenience. And just because he was a tycoon, used to making people jump, he needn't think that he was going to make her jump, too.

Harry made it to the airport in record time and found, of all things, a parking spot close to the terminal. It had to have something to do with driving a Rolls, Maureen thought with faint humor. Harry went with her into the airport and they met Jake, coming down the concourse toward her with new lines on his broad, dark face.

Maureen felt her heart jump wildly at the sight of him. Their relationship was still new to her, despite the fact that they'd been intimate and were married. Just seeing him was enough to make her body sing. Even her mind delighted in him. He was wearing a slate-gray business suit, very expensive, with a neat red-and-gray pinstriped tie, and he looked terribly handsome. Maureen, in her soft gray dress, with her hair in an elaborate coiffure and her face carefully made up, felt more presentable than she had in a long time. But he gave her only a cursory glance, his dark eyes going past her to Harry.

"I hope you found a space close by. I'm damned tired," he told the chauffeur, handing him the luggage strap. Harry nodded politely, turned around and began to pull the suitcase along on its wheels, discreetly leaving the boss and his new wife alone.

"How are you?" Maureen asked, her voice cool and stilted—not at all the voice of a new bride meeting her husband of several days.

He noticed that and hated the way things had gone between them. He wished he'd never spoken to her so coldly the day he'd left for Chicago. He should have taken her with him and tried to make up to her for leaving her practically at the altar to take care of business. Looking back, he knew he'd made a monumental mistake in tactics. She was going to be uneasy and distrustful of him from now on, and it was all his own fault. In fact, he'd been miserable the whole time he'd been gone. He'd missed her terribly during the past few days, and all his regrets were sitting on his broad shoulders as he looked down at her pale, miserable face. He'd bullied her into marriage without giving her time to get her breath, and then expected her to go on as if nothing had happened. He hadn't even kissed her goodbye, much less made love to her.

He couldn't blame her for the lost, sad look on her face. He'd put it there with his fear of being tied, of being possessed by her. He hadn't quite realized what marriage was going to mean until it was too late to back out. It had taken him a few days to accept those ties, but Maureen didn't know that. Now he was going to have to show her that he didn't resent her presence in his life. But it wasn't going to be easy; her attitude told him that.

"How am I? I'm tired," he said quietly. "But I'm all right. How about you?"

She couldn't quite meet his eyes. "I'm fine, too."

He shifted, wishing he had the right words to undo the damage he'd done. His big hand reached out and touched her cheek lightly. "Suppose you and I go and look for a house today?"

She hesitated. She wasn't sure whether or not they had a future together, but at least it was a kind of peace offering. It might get them on a better footing. "All right," she replied, but she backed away, because the feel of his fingers on her soft skin was disturbing.

He misread that move and dropped his hand without making an issue of her withdrawal. She was entitled, he thought bitterly. His face closed up. "We'll swing by the office," he said as he started back down the crowded walkway. "I have to leave some papers there."

She felt driven to try to calm the atmosphere between them. "What kind of house do you want?" she asked.

He shrugged. "Something with doors and windows, I suppose."

She couldn't help the smile that touched her mouth. "And a kitchen? I can cook, remember...."

"You won't. I told you, I want a French chef." He glanced at her. "A house the size we're going to buy will be too much for you by yourself. You'll find things to do. Before you know it, all your days will be full."

And what about the nights? she wanted to ask. But that would be asking for trouble.

She pushed back a strand of loose hair. "So I'm going to be a figurehead, is that right? A decorative item? Fine. Then you can buy me a new wardrobe and have my hair styled and—"

"Oh, hell," he muttered roughly. "That isn't what I meant at all. But if you want a wardrobe, go and buy one. You can have the charge card whenever you want it."

"Thank you," she said sweetly. She walked quickly to keep up with him. "And furthermore, I'm not giving up my job."

He stopped short. "I beg your pardon?"

The look didn't work as it was meant to. "You won't intimidate me by glaring at me," she returned. "I won't quit my job. If you won't let me be a wife, I'll be a career woman."

"You can't manage a house the size of the one I'm going to buy all by yourself," he said through his teeth.

"Watch me," she challenged. "Either you let me do it, or so help me, I'll keep working and I won't live with you!"

He took a slow breath. "You're a first-class pain in the neck!"

"Look who's talking!"

He glared and she glared back. Neither of them gave an inch, until the absurdity of the situation got through to Jake and he started chuckling. She was spirited. He hadn't realized that she had a temper because, until now, she'd been rather shy and withdrawn with him most of the time. But spirit wasn't a drawback. It was more like a bonus. She might manage to fit into his world after all, if she had spunk.

"You needn't laugh at me," she retorted.

"I'm not laughing. Not quite, anyway." He pursed his chiseled lips and stared down at her. "Okay. Try keeping the house by yourself, if that's how you want it. We'll see if you can manage."

She grinned, delighted at having her way. "I'll do very well," she replied. "I like cooking and cleaning."

"I'll remind you that you said that," he mused and started walking again. She was used to a small apartment. He didn't think she had any idea of the kind of house they were about to move into. But he'd let her find out for herself.

"Anyway, if we had a houseful of help, you'd have to buy me a gong. Isn't that what society hostesses use to ring for each course?" She smiled to herself. "I'd rather have a tuba and start my own tradition."

He laughed softly. He'd been very somber while he was away, but Maureen made him smile. She was the only woman who ever had. "I wouldn't mind," he said easily, escorting her out to the Rolls, where Harry was holding the door open. "As long as you don't paint your hair orange," he added and laughed at her expression.

They pulled away from the curb and Maureen's eye was caught by two young women, smiling at the Rolls with fascination and envy. She wondered what fantasies they were building about the wealthy man and woman in a Rolls-Royce.

Harry drove them around the best residential areas and past several For Sale signs until one caught Jake's eye and he had Harry stop in front of a two-story gray marble house.

It was set on beautifully landscaped grounds, and there was a garage and a tennis court.

"Ten bedrooms at least and servants' quarters out-back, if I'm not mistaken," Jake remarked. "Do you like it?"

Maureen was stunned. Somehow she hadn't considered ten bedrooms a necessity. But he was probably used to people coming to visit and to stay—business associates. And now she began to have some idea of the magnitude of the household chores she'd insisted on taking over. She wished she'd kept her mouth shut, but she was too proud to go back on her promise now.

The house was very nice. She knew this section of Wichita, and it was where the wealthy lived. She was used to a secretary's paycheck and living on a shoestring. Just the thought of high-society entertaining gave her hives. But she could do it. She had to. The success of their marriage would depend on her adjusting to his way of life.

She looked up at him as they stood in the foyer with the real-estate agent, a very sophisticated redhead who seemed awed by Jake's good looks and take-charge manner.

Maureen was shocked at the wave of possessiveness that washed over her, but she didn't dare let Jake see it. He didn't want a clinging, possessive wife. So she wandered off by herself to look around while the other woman hung on Jake's every word as he outlined what he wanted done about the house.

The big stone fireplace in the living room fascinated Maureen. She could almost see and smell a roaring fire there in winter, and she pictured herself and Jake sitting near it, talking, with her head on his shoulder and his arm around her. She sighed. That would take some doing, with him all over the world on business. A more realistic picture would be herself here, perhaps with a child in her arms.

That thought melted her. She leaned against the door with a wistful, soft smile on her face. A little boy, perhaps. A tiny little boy in one of those fleecy, footed pajamas with his hands curled around a bottle....

"It does look heavenly, doesn't it?" the realtor said with a sigh, joining her with Jake just behind. "I'd adore a white fur rug in front of it, and the right man beside me with the flames leaping in the hearth," she added throatily.

He was watching Maureen's averted face curiously. "What were you picturing, Maureen?" he asked suddenly.

She sighed, still looking at the fireplace without weighing the wisdom of the answer that came immediately to her tongue. "Oh, I was thinking about children," she murmured absently.

Jake's face underwent a remarkable change. It softened, like his dark eyes, and the look he sent toward his oblivious wife made the realtor clear her throat and start spouting prices and the advantages of the location.

Maureen turned around, stunned by the agent's quick change of attitude. Her eyes met Jake's and she felt the impact of his stare right through her. Those dark eyes went to her stomach, and she realized belatedly what he was thinking. She flushed and one quick jerk of her head told him what he wanted to know. Something seemed to flicker and die in his dark eyes. He shrugged and turned back to the hall without a word.

She wandered through the huge study and the smaller library, trailing behind him and the realtor, frowning at his behavior. Had he wanted her to be pregnant? Surely not, when he was talking about being away most of the time. If he'd really wanted children, he'd have been thinking of ways to be near them. No, it was probably just a stray thought, one he was already regretting. Now he knew there wasn't going to be a child, and he probably wished he hadn't rushed into marriage before he found out. She didn't know how to read him anymore. She'd thought she knew the mechanic named Jake, but the tycoon was another question entirely.

At the end of the tour, Jake said tersely that they'd take the house, without even consulting Maureen. Which did absolutely nothing to melt the ice that was growing between them.

All the way back to her apartment, she smoldered. By the time they reached it, she was all but boiling over.

Jake took the bag from Harry and sent him off. Then he turned to Maureen as she started coldly toward her own apartment.

"Like hell you do," he said shortly.

He caught her arm, leaving his luggage under the carport, and held on to her while he unlocked the door of his apartment and pulled her inside.

"Would you mind telling me— Oh!"

He cut her off with the hard pressure of his mouth. While he kissed her, his hand reached behind to lock the door. Then she was up in his arms and he was carrying her.

"Heaven," he breathed against her trembling mouth. "Oh, God, it's sheer heaven!"

She felt that way, too, but she didn't have enough breath to say it. He tossed her roughly into the middle of his bed and looked down at her while his hands went slowly to the buttons of his jacket.

She lay looking up at him half-dazed. It had all happened so suddenly. "Are you showing me my place?" she asked quietly. "Is this where I'm going to fit into your life? A pleasant diversion between business deals and office work?"

His big hands stilled on his shirt buttons. He stared down at her with quiet eyes. "You haven't forgotten what I said to you before I left."

"It isn't likely that I could," she replied. "Go ahead, if you want me," she said stiffly. "I'm your wife. This is my duty, and I'll do it."

"Oh, my God, not like this!" he ground out. "Don't make sex into a business arrangement!"

"Isn't that what it is to you?" she asked quietly. She sat up, feeling shaky even if she didn't sound it. "You married me because you wanted me. At the time, I thought you might . . . might care for me a little, but you disabused me of that idea the day we got married. You told me just how it was going to be. You liked being with me, and you liked sleeping with me, but business and the corporation came first." She stared at her hands in her lap and noticed a faint chip on one nail. She picked at it nervously. "If you'd stopped to think about it, you'd never have married me. I'm as different from you as night is from day. You don't like the way I look or the way I dress, and you don't think I've got the breeding to entertain your friends."

She looked up, suddenly, and caught the expression on his face. It made her cringe inside. "I'm right, aren't I!" she asked miserably. Tears filled her green eyes. She took her glasses off and dabbed at the tears with the hem of her dress. "Why don't you get an annulment? I'm not pregnant, so you don't have to worry about a child. We can go our own ways with no damage done, and next time you can marry someone who suits you better."

He didn't know what to say. He felt helpless, which made him angry. He moved away from her to light a cigarette. "I don't want an annulment," he said shortly. "I want you, warts and all."

"No, you don't," she said. "You want the idea of a wife and family, but you aren't willing to devote any time to either."

"I'm thirty-seven years old," he said shortly, turning to face her with narrow dark eyes. "I've never even lived with a woman. I've never had to answer to anyone. My time has always been my own, and business has filled it."

"Children need two parents," she said simply. "And I don't want to wind up like so many society wives do—with a drinking habit or a lover because I'm left alone too much."

"I can't give you all my time," he said.

"I'm not asking for it," she replied. "I just want more than an occasional hour in bed and being made to feel like a harem girl."

He stared at her levelly. "Is that how I made you feel the first time we made love together?"

She colored and lowered her eyes to his broad chest where his shirt was unbuttoned and thick hair peeked out of the opening. "Oh, no," she confessed huskily. "You made me feel the way every woman dreams of feeling, her first time."

"Do you really think I'd have given a damn about your pleasure if I were the kind of man you're trying to make me out to be?"

"You're twisting it," she muttered.

"No, you are." He came closer, kneeling just in front of her, one big hand on her thigh while the other idly held the burning cigarette. Pungent smoke rose between them. "I want to live with you. I can't guarantee you the moon, or that I'll be home on time every night. But I'll take care of you, and I swear on my heart that you'll never be just a body in bed to me."

"But you don't love me," she whispered miserably. "You just want me."

"For a man, wanting sometimes comes first. It's the way we're made." He smoothed his hand over her thigh, watching the material of her dress ripple sensuously under his fingers. "You want me just as badly. I can hear your breathing change when I touch you."

"Yes, but..."

"But what?" He moved, easing her backward so that she was lying down, and his big body slid sinuously over her, pressing her down into the mattress.

"Your... cigarette," she gasped as his hips settled over hers.

"To hell with the cigarette." His mouth went down on hers.

Somewhere along the way, the cigarette wound up in an ashtray and their clothing scattered from the bed to the floor. Maureen felt his skin brushing hers, the thick hair on his chest abrasive on her bare breasts, his mouth smoky and expertly demanding on the swelling contours of her soft lips.

She clung to him, moaning softly at the things he did to her, glorying in the sweet pleasure of loving. He whispered to her, graphic things, touching her in remembered ways, guiding her own hands, leading her deeper and deeper into the high waves of passion.

When she felt him lift her, her eyes opened, drowsy and narrow, to look straight up into his.

He held her gaze while his powerful body slowly, sensually, overwhelmed hers and she gasped at the stark intrusion, at the fusion that made her fantasies about him shatter under the blinding pleasure. He knew so much, she thought, crying out as the sensations piled one up on another and began to throb in great red waves. He knew... everything!

He laughed roughly, watching her helpless response to him, feeling her nails stabbing into his hips, her body lift to his as fulfillment buffeted her damp body. She cried out, the same throb in her voice that he felt in the pliant body beneath his. He watched her face as it happened to her, and only then gave himself the freedom to dive into the ecstasy with her. The waves hit him, too, and he groaned and groaned, his deep voice twining with her sharp cries as he felt the world spin off into darkness around him.

She couldn't stop crying. He held her, shuddering in his own peace, and smoothed her damp hair away from her wet face.

"It's all right," he whispered. His lips touched her eyelids, sipping away the salty tears. "It's all right, now."

But still she cried, her arms clinging around his neck, her body trembling as it sought the powerful contours of his, sought comfort.

His big hands smoothed down her back, loving the warmth of her. "I watched you," he whispered against her lips. "It was better this time than last."

"Oh, yes," she moaned, shivering. Her face burrowed into his damp throat, feeling the throbbing coolness of his skin. "Don't let go."

"I won't." He rolled onto his side, easing her lovingly against him, caressing her with his lips and his hands. "Is it easing?"

"N-no," she choked. "I'm sorry, I... Jake!" Her nails bit into him and she arched in sweet anguish as he moved over her, against her, his mouth grinding into hers as he shifted.

"Easy now," he whispered into her mouth. "Come closer. I won't let you go until you feel it completely, this time. Kiss me...."

She hadn't realized that it was possible to survive such an explosion of sensation. She clung to him, spinning wildly between heaven and earth while he made the world go red with a completion beyond her wildest dreams. It was the closest she'd come to a dead faint, and she couldn't even lift her head when she felt him move slowly away from her at last.

"Come here, baby," he whispered. He gathered her to him and pillowed her head on his shuddering chest. He stretched, groaning. "My God, I think I'm going to die of muscle failure. Are you all right?"

"If I die, right now, it will be all right," she whispered on a shaky sigh. "I love you, Jake."

"I'd have to be blind not to know it now," he murmured softly, smiling against her soft mouth.

"You don't mind?" she asked quietly.

His head moved against her cheek. "I don't mind. It just takes some getting used to, that's all." He laughed bitterly. "I've never been loved. Not by anyone."

She framed his broad face with her hands and held it so that she could see his dark, haunted eyes. "Your parents..."

"I was adopted. Haven't you guessed?" he asked coldly. "They wanted children, or so they thought, so they adopted me from a young unwed mother whose name I never learned. When I got into trouble with the law, they blamed it on my unknown parentage and literally washed their hands of me."

She couldn't quite take it all in. "But you inherited the corporation?"

"My adoptive father hadn't changed his will, for God alone knows what reason. My mother had an income for her lifetime, but the corporation went to me." He rolled over onto his back, magnificent in his nudity, and laughed coldly. "You can't imagine how she hated that. She couldn't get a penny out of me. She drank. And when she drank, she liked to call me and tell me what a hell I'd made of her life when I was a child. She'd get into the damnedest messes and call me to fly overseas and get her out of them. I cursed her until I ran out of curses, until the very night she died trying to kill me."

"Oh, Jake." She moved close to him, holding him, her cheek nestled on his hair-roughened chest. "Everyone said that you loved her, and I thought... I don't know what I thought. I'm so sorry."

"I wanted to love her," he said heavily. "But she wasn't the kind of woman who wanted that." He smoothed the arm that lay across him. "She really hated me. I never quite knew why, unless she and my father had a warped idea of what parenthood meant. I think they realized at last that children aren't amusing little dolls that can be put on a shelf and forgotten when they aren't wanted."

"That's true," she said quietly. "But neither are wives."

He lifted his head and looked down at her. "I don't know very much about wives. I never wanted one, until you came along. I don't know much about children, either. But I suppose you and I can learn together."

"Can you spare the time?"

He sighed and touched her breasts gently with the tips of his fingers, watching her tautening body. "Oh, I think I'll manage that." His dark eyes caught hers. "Say it again."

"I . . . I love you," she choked, arching toward his fingers.

"How much?"

"More than anyone or anything in the world," she managed as his mouth came down to hers. "Except . . ."

His lips poised just over hers, his excited breath making cool shivers against them, "Except?" he asked, his tone challenging.

She lifted her hands to the back of his head. "Except for the child I'm going to give you . . . nine months from today," she breathed shakily and brought his lips over hers.

He shuddered, and then his arms gathered her up tightly and he gave in, for the first time, to the need to be loved.

Eleven

Maureen and Jake bought the big gray house, and she did give up her job. But if Jake had thought she wouldn't be able to cope, he was wrong.

She found books on hostessing and other books on estate management. She took advantage of Jake's first overseas trip to start taking the reins of the household in hand. She hired a cook—not a French chef, but a kindly retired lady with an exquisite repertoire of home cookery—and a housekeeper and a maid. She employed a gardener. She went shopping for just the right clothes and had her hair done by an expert. The only concession she didn't make was to give up her glasses—she kept them, because after so many years, they felt like part of her.

"Mr. MacFaber is due home today, isn't he, Mrs. MacFaber?" Mrs. Candles, the cook, asked. "What shall I make?"

"Chicken crepes," she said instantly. "He loves those. And a potato casserole, asparagus, and a small caramel pudding for desert," Maureen told her with a smile. "That should satisfy his hunger for French cuisine and mine for American. Oh, and could you make a big chef's salad as well?"

"Yes, ma'am." Mrs. Candles grinned. "Wine?"

"I'll have coffee and so will Mr. MacFaber," she murmured. "I want him to keep a clear head so that he can see the changes around here."

The cook went away shaking her head.

Maureen had a gorgeous crepe dress with an overlay of hand-painted chiffon in rainbow colors. She wore that, with its billowing skirt, and left her hair loose in waves that fell beautifully to her shoulders. She didn't look the epitome of a sophisticated tycoon's wife, but she did look like Jake MacFaber's wife, she consoled herself.

He came in the door just as she came down the stairs, and Clare, the new maid, was quick to take his briefcase and raincoat.

"It was coming down in buckets in New York," Jake murmured, his eyes following the neat little maid's progress. He looked up at Maureen and his lips pursed as his dark eyes slid over her hungrily. "Are you going to be dessert?" he asked huskily.

"If you'd rather have me than a caramel pudding with cream," she said, laughing. "Oh, Jake, I missed you so!"

She threw herself into his arms, to be swung around and kissed within an inch of her life. He'd been gone for three weeks, and she'd barely been able to stand being away from him, even though he'd phoned almost every day. It wasn't the same as having him close in her arms like this.

"Are you going to kiss me to death?" he whispered.

"Can I try?" She grinned and reached up to his mouth again.

"I'm not complaining." He nuzzled his cheek against hers with a heavy sigh and brought her close, his body shuddering a little. "I need you, Maureen," he whispered at her ear. "Suppose we make love on the hall table?"

"Mrs. Candles would faint."

He lifted his head, frowning. "Mrs. Who? And come to think of it, who was that?" He nodded in the direction in which the maid had gone.

"Clare is our maid," she explained. "Mrs. Candles is our chef."

His heavy brows began to knit. "Is she a French chef?"

"Her great-grandfather was French," she assured him. "And she's a top-notch chef."

"Now, listen, baby..."

She took his hand and pulled him along. "We can go to bed early," she promised, "and I'll show you how much I missed you. But right now, you have to taste Mrs. Candles's crepes!"

He allowed himself to be persuaded, but he was still reluctant, right up until he took the first mouthful of Mrs. Candles's crepes. Then Maureen could see all his resistance crumbling.

"Marvelous," he said.

"Yes, isn't it?" Maureen grinned. "We also have a gardener, and I have a new wardrobe, and we're giving a dinner party next week for all your executives at the corporation."

He blinked, shocked by her take-charge manner. "Well, well, you've been a busy little bee, haven't you?" he mused.

"Indeed I have," she said, laughing.

His eyes narrowed. "You haven't been sneaking back to the office to work?"

"I don't have time for that these days," she murmured. "I've been too busy looking after the house and getting everything organized. Do you like to swim?"

He stared at her. "Yes," he said cautiously.

"Good."

There was a sudden *whump* in the backyard.

"What was that?!" he burst out and started to get up.

She touched his hand gently, easing him back down. "Nothing to get excited about. It's just the bulldozer."

"What bulldozer?"

"The one that's digging the hole for the swimming pool," she explained calmly. "Do eat your crepe, sweetheart. It's going to get cold."

He let out a slow breath, frowning toward the noise outback. "Are there any more surprises in store for me?" he asked.

"Only one little one," she said carelessly. "But not right away. Don't you want some potato casserole?"

"I don't think I like potato casserole," he said absently. "My God, you haven't wasted any time, have you?" he chuckled. "Maids, housekeepers... And I thought you couldn't cope. More fool, me."

"You didn't realize how desperately I love you, that's all," she said, smiling softly at him, her eyes adoring on his dark face. "When you love someone, you'll do anything to please them."

"Is that so?" he said, as his eyes twinkled mischievously. "Well, I do have an idea or two on that subject. When we've had dessert."

"So do I." She smoothed her fingers over his big hand, loving the very texture of it. Her hand slid into his and she clasped it warmly. "Jake," she said hesitantly, meeting his eyes. "Joseph," she corrected, and all the playfulness went out of her face. "I'm carrying your child."

At first she didn't think he'd heard her. He just sat staring at her. He didn't even seem to move. His eyes got wider, and darker, and the big hand in hers began to contract with growing hunger.

"You're what?" he asked huskily.

She smiled, and then she laughed. "I'm pregnant!"

"My God. My God!" He came around the table, laughing, scooped her up and sat down with her in his lap. "When? How long?"

"A little over six months from now," she sighed, nuzzling her face against him. "I wanted to be sure before I told you, and I wasn't until I saw the doctor yesterday."

"We've been married a little over three months," he murmured, counting back. Then he grinned and she colored. "Just about," he breathed, brushing his mouth over hers, "the afternoon you whispered something about nine months . . ."

"Hush!" She laughed, then reached up and kissed him, stilling the words on his lips.

A long moment later, a discreet cough parted them. They looked up, blank-faced, as Mrs. Candles set the pudding on the table.

She smiled at their blank looks. "Pudding," she explained. "It's healthy stuff. Great for blossoming parents."

"However did you know?" Maureen gasped.

Mrs. Candles grinned. "I had six of my own, didn't I tell you? I'll just bring the cream in, then I'll go to my room and watch television."

Jake chuckled as she left. "She's terrific," he murmured. "And much more pleasant than a temperamental French chef throwing things about in the kitchen."

"Darling, if you miss that, I'm sure Mrs. Candles could throw a pot now and again, just to make you feel comfortable."

"No need," he murmured against her mouth. "We're going to be too busy to notice. Aren't we?"

Six months later, Joshua Blake MacFaber came home from the hospital in his father's arms while his mother was gently eased from the car and into a wheelchair for the trip inside. It had been a difficult birth, ending in a cesarean section, but Maureen was so proud of their little boy that she hadn't minded the discomfort one bit.

"Isn't he the image of his father?" she asked Mrs. Candles as they brought him inside.

"Indeed he is, madam," the cook replied, smiling at the tiny bundle MacFaber was holding close against his heart. "Right down to his eyes. They'll be dark, you can tell."

Once Maureen was in bed, and little Joshua was curled up in her arms asleep, Jake offered to take him.

"You need to baby that incision along," he whispered as he lifted the tiny little boy in his big arms and sat down in the chair by the bed.

"Do I really?" she teased, her eyes glowing with love. "Or do you just like holding your son?"

"A bit of both." He touched the tiny sleeping face, and a wave of love so fierce that it made his cheeks ruddy washed over him. "My God, he's a miracle," he breathed.

"Yes." Maureen reached out, grimacing as the incision pulled, and touched Jake's hand where it rested on the child's body over the soft blanket. "I love you, darling," she whispered. "Thank you for sticking it out with me."

For he'd been there every second through her long labor, right up until the time they'd wheeled her into surgery. They'd prepared for natural childbirth, but something had gone wrong at the last minute.

"He's mine, too," he reminded her. His hand curled around hers and his eyes darkened. "Like you."

"You aren't sorry you married me?" she teased sleepily.

"I'm sorry it took me so long to find you," he replied, and he wasn't laughing. His eyes softened as he looked at her tired face. "I've never said the words, have I?" he asked quietly. "Not even when we made love."

"You wouldn't have stayed with me if you hadn't cared a little," she replied evasively.

His fingers edged between hers and he looked at her entwined hands and at their little boy, sleeping so peacefully in his arms. "I had to learn what love was before I could feel it, or express it," he said simply. "I learned that it's selfless. It puts the other person's feelings first, the other person's needs first. It never demands, it only accepts." He lifted his dark, steady eyes to hers. "Gibran said that love can't be directed, that if it finds you worthy, it directs *your* course." His fingers contracted around hers while her heart ran wild. "Will it shock you to learn that it's been directing my course for quite some time now, Maureen?"

Her lips parted. "It shouldn't," she confessed. "But I think it does. You're so private...."

"I love you," he said gruffly, his eyes blazing with it. "Deathlessly. Obsessively. I don't even know when it became love, but I know when I realized it. It was the day I came back from Chicago and you met me at the airport. You looked as if I'd hit you, and I felt sick at the things I'd said. I'd missed you so terribly, and I couldn't even tell you. Then we went back to my apartment, after we'd bought the house." He smiled wickedly. "And I told you something I'd never told anyone. That was when you made love to me. And somewhere in the middle of it, I knew that you were my world."

She colored at the sweetness of the memory and her fingers curled lovingly around his. "I knew that about you from the very beginning, Mr. MacFaber." She smiled. "Even if I didn't know your name, you've been my world since the first time I saw you."

"Maybe life would have been less complicated if I'd been that mechanic."

"It would have. But I don't love you any less as you truly are." She touched their son's sleeping face. "And he won't, either. You'll be his whole world, too."

He had to swallow twice before he could answer her. It was new, to admit love and hear it spoken of so openly. But he liked it. He liked it very much.

He lifted dark eyes to hers and smiled. "I guess it's a good thing that I've delegated some authority at the corporation, then, isn't it?" he murmured. "Things are going to be a lot less complicated from now on. I'll have an occasional trip out of town, but I'll be home most nights and on weekends."

"Jake!"

"Shocked? I told you. I love you. I can't very well be a proper husband and father if I'm never home."

"But the corporation . . ."

"Is no longer my life," he said simply. He brought her hand to his mouth and kissed it hungrily. "You are," he said, and the tone of his voice made her skin tingle.

"We can go on picnics," she whispered. "And have birthday parties for Joshua."

"And his brothers and sisters," he added with a purely masculine glitter in his dark eyes.

She caught her breath, and her own eyes began to sparkle. "Oh, darling!" she whispered.

"There's just one thing," he said, and he looked so somber that Maureen felt apprehensive.

"What?" she asked worriedly.

"Could you please ask Mrs. Candles to stop making chicken crepes?"

"But it's your favorite dish!" she exclaimed.

"It was, until we had it every night for two weeks," he said through his teeth.

She burst out laughing. "I'll save you, don't worry. We'll never have chicken crepes again."

"Good."

"We'll have beef crepes instead."

He started to say something, but young Joshua moved and opened his tiny eyes. And the playful banter got lost somewhere in the wonder of two new parents looking at their infant son.

*   *   *   *   *

MAURA SEGER

A compelling trilogy stretching from the Civil War to the twentieth century and chronicling the lives of three passionate women.

SARAH is the story of an independent woman's fight for freedom during the Civil War and her love for the one man who kindles her pride and passion. $3.95 ☐

ELIZABETH, set in the aftermath of the Civil War, is the tale of a divided nation's struggle to become one and two tempestuous hearts striving for everlasting love. $3.95 ☐

CATHERINE chronicles the love story of an upper-class beauty and a handsome Irishman in turn-of-the-century Boston. $3.95 U.S. ☐
$4.50 Cdn. ☐

Total Amount $ _____
Plus 75¢ Postage .75
Payment enclosed $ _____

1989
IS THE YEAR OF THE MAN!

What makes a romance? A special man, of course, and Silhouette Desire celebrates that fact with *twelve* of them! From Mr. January to Mr. December, every month has a tribute to the Silhouette Desire hero—our **MAN OF THE MONTH!**

Sexy, macho, charming, irritating . . . irresistible! Nothing can stop these men from sweeping you away. Created by some of your favorite authors, each man is custom-made for pleasure—*reading* pleasure—so don't miss a single one.

Mr. January is Blake Donavan in RELUCTANT FATHER by Diana Palmer
Mr. February is Hank Branson in THE GENTLEMAN INSISTS by Joan Hohl
Mr. March is Carson Tanner in NIGHT OF THE HUNTER by Jennifer Greene
Mr. April is Slater McCall in A DANGEROUS KIND OF MAN by Naomi Horton
Mr. May is Luke Harmon in VENGEANCE IS MINE by Lucy Gordon
Mr. June is Quinn McNamara in IRRESISTIBLE by Annette Broadrick

And that's only the half of it— so get out there and find your man!

Silhouette Desire's
MAN OF THE MONTH . . .

MOM-1

Silhouette Classics

COMING IN APRIL...

THORNE'S WAY by Joan Hohl

When *Thorne's Way* first burst upon the romance scene in 1982, readers couldn't help but fall in love with Jonas Thorne, a man of bewildering arrogance and stunning tenderness. This book quickly became one of Silhouette's most sought-after early titles.

Now, Silhouette Classics is pleased to present the reissue of *Thorne's Way*. Even if you read this book years ago, its depth of emotion and passion will stir your heart again and again.

And that's not all!

Silhouette Special Edition

COMING IN JULY...

THORNE'S WIFE by Joan Hohl

We're pleased to announce a truly unique event at Silhouette. Jonas Thorne is back, in *Thorne's Wife*, a sequel that will sweep you off your feet! Jonas and Valerie's story continues as life—and love—reach heights never before dreamed of.

Experience both these timeless classics—one from Silhouette Classics and one from Silhouette Special Edition—as master storyteller Joan Hohl weaves two passionate, dramatic tales of everlasting love!

CL-36

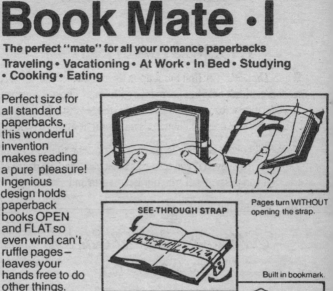

Silhouette Special Edition®

NAVY BLUES
Debbie Macomber

Between the devil and the deep blue sea...

At Christmastime, Lieutenant Commander Steve Kyle finds his heart anchored by the past, so he vows to give his ex-wife wide berth. But Carol Kyle is quaffing milk and knitting tiny pastel blankets with a vengeance. She's determined to have a baby, and only one man will do as father-to-be—the only man she's ever loved...her own bullheaded ex-husband!

You met Steve and Carol in NAVY WIFE (Special Edition #494)—you'll cheer for them in NAVY BLUES (Special Edition #518). (And as a bonus for NAVY WIFE fans, newlyweds Rush and Lindy Callaghan reveal a surprise of their own....)

Each book stands alone—together they're Debbie Macomber's most delightful duo to date! Don't miss

**NAVY BLUES
Available in April,
only in *Silhouette Special Edition*.
Having the "blues" was never
so much fun!**

Silhouette Intimate Moments®

Let Bestselling Author KATHLEEN EAGLE Sweep You Away to De Colores Once Again

For the third time, Kathleen Eagle has written a book set on the spellbinding isle of De Colores. In PAINTBOX MORNING (Intimate Moments #284), Miguel Hidalgo is all that stands between his island home and destruction—and Ronnie Harper is the only woman who can help Miguel fulfill his destiny and lead his people into a bright tomorrow. But Ronnie has a woman's heart, a woman's needs. In helping Miguel to live out his dreams, is she destined to see her own dreams of love with this very special man go forever unfulfilled? Read PAINTBOX MORNING, coming this month from Silhouette Intimate Moments, and follow the path of these star-crossed lovers as they build a future filled with hope and a love to last all time.

If you like PAINTBOX MORNING, you might also like Kathleen Eagle's two previous tales of De Colores: CANDLES IN THE NIGHT (Special Edition #437) and MORE THAN A MIRACLE (Intimate Moments #242).

For your copy, send $2.75 plus 75¢ postage and handling to:

In USA

901 Furhmann Blvd.
P.O. Box 1396
Buffalo, NY 14269-1396

In Canada

P.O. Box 609
Fort Erie, Ontario
L2A 5X3

Please specify book title with your order.

IM284-1A